
The shifting of the mattress woke me.
I reached up and touched her smooth, bare back. She flinched and swung around.

"Someone's in the house!"

And then I heard the steps in the hall outside. It was that awful, endless moment out of time, when you know something terrible is going to happen, and there is nothing you can do but wait.

The door opened. I saw two figures, heard an exclamation, and at once the room burst into light.

Tony stood in the doorway. The flat, light-brown eyes fell on us, and the creases of his cruel grin settled around his mouth. Behind him stood the kid, his hair hanging in dark, greasy bangs over his eyes. He was grinning, too. I saw what he held in his right hand.

He had a gun, now pointed carelessly at the floor. It wasn't a little .32 like the one I had threatened Tony with. It was a .44 magnum revolver. It is not a gun for impressing people. It is for killing. . . .

DEATH IN
CONNECTICUT

David Linzee

A DELL BOOK

Published by
DELL PUBLISHING CO., INC.
1 Dag Hammarskjold Plaza
New York, N.Y. 10017

Dell ® TM 681510, Dell Publishing Co., Inc.

ISBN: 0-440-12298-8

Reprinted by arrangement with
David McKay Company, Inc. / Ives Washburn, Inc.

Printed in the United States of America

First Dell printing—November 1978

PART ONE

1

It took me a long time to decide which gun to use.

I looked through the latticed glass. In the dark recesses of the cabinet, the four shotgun barrels gave a chilly gleam. I swung open the heavy door and reached for the venerable .16 gauge that was my father's favorite.

I pictured the moment: I would pull off the road and move over to the passenger seat. Then I would slide the shotgun down between my knees, lean over till the cold rim pressed against my forehead, stretch my hand down for the trigger. . . .

Would I be able to reach the trigger? Perhaps I should sit down now and try it. I wanted no delays when the moment came.

But I did not sit. I stared at the shotgun, thinking, then put it back and crossed the study to the desk.

I found what I was looking for in the bottom drawer, resting on a bed of erasers and memo pads that read, *From the desk of Arthur Lavien, Sr.:* an old .32 revolver with a four-inch barrel. I picked it up; the blued surface was freckled with rust. It was not one of my father's hunting guns, and he didn't care much about it. That stopped me for a moment: I had planned on using his favorite. . . .

I hesitated only a moment before slamming the drawer shut and standing with the revolver in my hand. How pathetic, to die in order to make someone feel guilty! He might feel twinges of uneasiness for a few months, but I would be dead forever. No, I was doing this for myself, and I would use the handgun because that would make it easier. I found the cartridges in another drawer, loaded two in the chambers, and left the study.

I called the garage from the living room, looking out the window as I dialed. Twenty-five stories below, the East River made its grim path to the sea, and beyond it the immense grey factories of Queens sprawled away mile after mile into the gathering dusk. There was only one touch of color in the scene: the red neon swirls of a Pepsi-Cola advertisement fastened to some smokestacks on the river's edge. For this view my father had paid fifty thousand dollars.

"Garage."

"This is Lavien in Twenty-five B. I'd like my car, please."

"Yes, Mr. Lavien. We'll have it at the door in a couple of minutes."

I put the phone back and started for the door. I felt calm, but my body knew that something fearful was going to be done to it. There was a tremor in my left leg, and cold drops of sweat trickled down my ribs. On impulse I stopped at the bar and grabbed a bottle of Chivas Regal. I would take courage wherever I could find it.

I slipped the gun into my pocket and went out.

2

Years before, when I was in high school and slogging through some required reading, I had come across a thought that really struck my adolescent mind. The heroine of this novel—I can't remember the title, but it was a very depressing book—is idly turning over the leaves of a calendar when a singular thought occurs to her: one of these pages bears the date on which, in some particular year, she will die. She goes through the pages again, expecting that one date to touch her with a premonitory chill. I was so impressed with this at the time that I got up and went to the calendar on our kitchen wall and began to turn the pages. As I recall, I felt no chill as I looked at April 21.

But April 21 it was to be. April 21, 1971.

It found me on the New Jersey Turnpike, riding beside a stranger. I was hitching from Ann Arbor to Washington. Or I thought I was; I had no idea then that I was going home. I just knew that it was spring, Nixon was President, and I felt mildly depressed.

I was beginning to worry about the guy who had picked me up, too. He was a balding, mild-faced man of about thirty; and he wore his tie straight and tight, even though he'd been driving all night, and had half a dozen pens and pencils in a plastic liner in his breast pocket. He told me he was "in critical path scheduling" at Sikorsky aircraft. I nodded and stared moodily at the American flag decal on his window, and wondered why he had picked up a long-haired hippie like me.

When he asked if I'd heard any good dirty jokes lately, I began to fear the worst.

I told him I hadn't. But he had, and I listened to them for the next twenty miles. Something about the way he looked sideways at me to see how I was taking it, and the fact that his knuckles were going white on the wheel, told me I was in for it.

"Hey," he said, "and something really wild happened last week to a guy I know."

He gave a little gasping laugh and glanced sideways at me. Here it comes, I thought.

"Yeah?" I edged closer to the door.

"He was hitchhiking, just like you, and this guy picked him up, and, well, he had this really wild proposition."

Another sideways glance. This time I didn't say anything, but he went on.

"He told my friend, 'I'll pay you twenty-five bucks if you'll let me give *you* a blow-job.' "

"How about that," I said. "Pretty wild, all right." I laughed, but the critical path scheduler was in earnest now.

"As a matter of fact, my friend thought that was a pretty good deal."

"No kidding. How about that."

There was a brief, terrible pause.

"So—uh—what would—what do you think you'd do in a situation like that?"

"You know," I said loudly, "this is a pretty nice car you got here."

"No, seriously. What would you say to a deal like that?"

"What kind of mileage do you get?"

Silence. I glanced at him. He was staring straight ahead, with a set, desperate expression.

"Listen, fellah, what I'm getting at is—"

"This is where I get off," I said, throwing off my seat belt.

"Here? There's nothing here."

"That's O.K."

"But I can't stop by the side of the road. It's against the law."

"There's a rest stop just ahead."

And there was, thank God. He was silent as we drove up the long entrance ramp. But as I turned to get out, he faced me with some dignity and said, "Sorry I got you wrong, fellah. You look like you could use twenty-five bucks."

And he pulled away.

I looked around me. The Alexander Hamilton Rest Stop stood on a slight hill, and I could look down on eight lanes of Jersey Turnpike. Beyond, the tanks and pipes and cranes of an oil refinery stretched away until they were swallowed up in the heavy yellow-grey air. New Jersey air. It looked as if just touching it would be unhealthy, and here I was breathing it.

I turned away from the unlovely prospect of the wasteland of capitalism and walked past the shoulder-high wheels of tractor-trailor rigs to the coffee shop. I went in through the glass doors and stood in the lobby, as far as I could get without being nailed by a waitress. Enviously I watched the truck drivers and salesmen digging into their scrambled eggs. My last meal had been a hamburger somewhere in Ohio. I had three and a half dollars in the world, and I felt like blowing it all on breakfast.

But I was too experienced for such a foolish indulgence—I had been a tramp for three years, after all.

So I went out through the glass doors, sat down on the curb, and tried to figure out what to do with the three and a half dollars. I would have to reach some city where I knew people and could crash for a while, until I could get a temporary job. I didn't know anybody in New Jersey, and I didn't want to go back to New York, for a lot of reasons. I started to calculate how long it would take me to reach Philly and turned to glance longingly at the restaurant. It would be a long, hungry day, even if I was lucky.

A man in a white shirt and tie was looking out the window at me. I got up; I knew that in a minute he would come out and tell me to move along. You didn't belong here if you didn't have a car.

As I walked aimlessly away, a thought slipped unbidden into my head: if you had twenty-five dollars now, you could eat breakfast and afford to take a bus to Philadelphia. And for a moment I considered whether I had made a mistake not to take the critical path scheduler's offer.

And suddenly I laughed out loud. It is almost a relief to know you have hit rock bottom. I would not sink lower than this.

I can't remember exactly when I decided to head home, but suddenly I was thinking of my father's house in Hartford, Connecticut, not all that far away. There I would find a whole closetful of clean shirts— from Brooks Brothers, no less—and scrambled eggs and soap and shampoo.

And socks. I had been wearing the same clothes for two weeks now, and I dreaded unlacing my boots. It was like opening an unearthed coffin. I had known the socks were past washing a month ago, but had not been able to afford a new pair. The same went for everything I had on. I had become the man I used to hate sitting next to on a bus.

At one time I had owned a whole knapsack full of clothes, but it had gone the way of my sleeping bag and everything else I had possessed: ripped off by innocent and anti-materialistic hippies.

What did I have to show for three years of looking for America? Well, there were warrants out for my arrest in four states: California for unlawful assembly, Colorado for fishing without a license, Illinois for hitchhiking, and Pennsylvania for driving a car with a burned-out taillight. And I had skipped bail in one of those places, too.

I looked at my boots, thinking again of those socks. Then I turned and went into the restaurant to call home.

And that was how I made the fatal decision: for want of a pair of clean socks. It was inevitable, I suppose: if you are broke enough and near enough to home, you go back. Whatever you're going to find.

I went in and placed a collect call to my father's office. There would be no one at home; my mother was dead.

"Good morning. Brian, Macon, and Watkins."

The secretary should have said, "Brian, Macon, and Lavien." My father was much more eminent than old Bill Watkins. Brian and Macon were the most eminent, being dead.

"Collect call from Mr. Arthur Levine," said the operator. "Will you accept charges?"

"Lavien," I said. "Junior."

"Who?" the secretary asked. She was very slow this morning.

"Arthur Lavien, Junior. Will you accept charges?"

"One moment."

The operator and I waited patiently. I remembered uneasily that my father had not heard from me in a year. I hadn't meant it that way, but under the circumstances writing to him was a little awkward.

The line opened and a new voice spoke.

"What name did you say?"

The voice sounded familiar. It also sounded unfriendly.

"Arthur Lavien. Er, Junior."

"Oh!" said the voice. "Yes, we'll accept charges."

"Thank you," and the operator's line closed.

"Arthur, this is Joanne Dean."

"Oh!" I said in turn. Joanne was my father's indispensable secretary. I had felt rather uneasy around her since I realized, about a month after my mother's death, that the old man was screwing her.

"Your father's not here any more. He's left the firm."

I wondered if he had left her as well.

"Where can I reach him?"

"He's left town, as a matter of fact."

Yes, he'd dropped her all right. My father would not go out of his way for a little sex.

"He's gone to Washington, I expect?"

Although my father lived in Hartford, he spent most of his time in Washington. He said this was helpful in his specialty, which he claimed was anti-trust law. Actually, it was essential to his specialty, which was Connections.

"No," said Joanne, "he's in New York now, with Maitland, Ruthven."

Maitland, Ruthven. That was even better than Washington. My father used to talk lovingly of New York, which he called "the fastest track," and of that particular firm. Maitland, Ruthven.

"Arthur? Still there?"

"Yes," I said. "So he finally made it, huh?"

"He finally made it."

A little bitterness there, on both sides.

"I guess—I guess you haven't been in contact with him much?"

"No," I answered, "but I'm going into the city now." And then I could not resist adding, "You don't see him much either?"

"He used to come up on weekends—he still keeps your old house."

"He does? He must be pretty loaded then?"

Joanne affirmed that, giving an involuntary sigh, perhaps at the thought of the weekends in Bermuda that were now going to some babe in New York.

I pressed it. A conversation about my father always brings out the vindictiveness in me.

"But he's stopped coming up on weekends?"

"Yes," said Joanne shortly, "long ago."

"Well, is there anything you'd like me to tell him when I see him?"

She hung up on me with a sharp click. I suppose that was my answer.

I replaced the phone and went out into the acrid, gritty air. I was glad he had moved to New York. That made my clean pair of socks a lot closer.

I walked down to the end of the entrance ramp and stuck out my thumb.

The very first car, a battered station wagon, slowed and eased toward me. Perhaps my luck was changing. But as I put out my hand for the door handle, it veered away and accelerated. I caught a glimpse of a fat, red-faced young man in a purple shirt, laughing at me through the window. As the car moved slowly away, he opened the door and leaned out, shouting a comment about my hair, adding doubts about my virility. I suppose he hoped I would give him and his friend the finger—and a chance to beat me up. But I didn't react, and they drove away. There was a FREE LT. CALLEY sticker on their back bumper.

I was glad I'd be through with this soon.

Finally I got a ride to New Brunswick, and there blew my three dollars on a bus ticket into the city. The Port Authority Terminal was hurried and dreary, as I had remembered it, and there were tough-looking black dudes at all the escalators, holding up papers and shouting, *"Black Panther Party News*—check it out." I shot one of them a V-sign, and he shot back at me a blank, hostile look. The sixties were over, all right.

I went out the doors to Eighth Avenue. Outside of New Jersey it was a pretty day. Tousled April clouds hurried along just beyond the reach of the West Side towers, and the sun came out from time to time in brief, golden gushes of light. There was a soft, warm breeze.

I walked a block north to avoid Forty-second Street and turned east. I told myself that I just wanted to take a look at the town again, but my eagerness for clean clothes and food had begun to fade as I mulled over that conversation with Joanne. It had reminded me what my father was like.

I turned onto Fifth Avenue and started walking uptown, away from Maitland, Ruthven. I noticed that I was passing a bank. Just beyond its glass wall, right on the first floor where everybody on the street could see it, was the door to the vault: highly polished steel, nearly a full story high. I stopped and looked at it.

Romances are supposed to begin on beaches or in peaceful parks, but mine had begun in front of a bank —this bank—on a May night four years ago, when Claire Cowan and I were seventeen.

We were walking back to Grand Central and our train to Hartford after a day in the city. It was dusk, soft and grey as the satin lining of a Tiffany's box. The Fifth Avenue merchants had closed up, leaving their broad sidewalks and the lights in their gorgeous windows to us alone. This bank, too, was lit from top to bottom, and Claire had looked at the brilliant vault door and grinned sardonically. "They're capitalists and proud of it, aren't they?"

I felt a thrill of solidarity. This, after all, was in 1967, when you would be told to go back to Russia if you referred to our glorious free enterprise system as "capitalism." I realized that this girl was on my side —and she was beautiful, too. I took her hand.

Claire didn't look at me but bent her elbow to draw my arm up under her coat and settle it around her waist. The movement was so natural, so matter-of-fact, as if we belonged to each other.

I wondered where she was today, as I had wondered every day for the past three years.

Maitland, Ruthven's building, stood in comforting proximity to Wall Street. It was a new one, a forty-story ice cube that had been jammed violently down between a pair of bulky, aging, concrete tombstones.

I half expected to be stopped in the lobby and told that I could not be admitted without a tie, but the single elevator attendant was off in a corner, chatting with a maintenance man. He didn't even look my way as I consulted the building directory.

The address of Maitland, Ruthven was simply 2100. They had a floor to themselves, of course. I found the right elevator and went up.

We used to play a game at school called "What My Father Does for a Living Is More Immoral Than What Your Father Does for a Living." I always won at that game. My father *was* the Establishment, the tie that bound Big Business and Big Government. He made a fortune seeing to it that the country was run the way the corporate elite wanted it run.

He used to tell my mother about his cases over dinner, and I remembered a typical one. A Hartford-based conglomerate that owned a chain of supermarkets wanted to take over a canning company in Rhode Island. Enter the Anti-Trust Division of the Department of Justice, with the tiresome complaint that this merger would tend toward the creation of a canned-vegetable monopoly in southern New England. My father grabbed his briefcase and headed for Washington. The next month I checked at the supermarket and found that creamed corn had gone up five cents a can.

The elevator doors opened onto a lobby of greenish marble veined in black. There were crisp block capitals on the wall opposite, proclaiming MAITLAND, RUTHVEN, LAVIEN, AND STEWART. He had made it, all right.

The receptionist was on the phone, writing down a message, and I spent an enjoyable moment looking at her. Her hair was long and dark, gathered loosely with a ribbon at the nape of her neck, and she had hazel eyes framed by arching brows and high, fine cheekbones. I wondered if she was Joanne's replacement.

"All right, thank you, sir," she said into the phone, put it down, and turned to me. Her smile wilted and died like a candle in a strong wind; ragged, dirty young men were an unusual sight at Maitland, Ruthven.

"Yes?" she said querulously. She knew I was going to be trouble, whatever I asked for.

I took a deep breath, fought a sudden urge to run out of the office, and said it.

"I'd like to see Mr. Lavien."

"I'm sorry," she said with relief. "Mr. Lavien is in Washington. If you'd care to leave a message—" She reached for a memo pad.

Of course. I had forgotten the salient fact of my relationship with ALsr (as he signed his memos): he was always in Washington.

The receptionist was looking at me with those fine hazel eyes; she had managed to put her smile back on.

"I'm Arthur Lavien," I said stupidly.

She gave me a blank look.

"I'm his son, Arthur Lavien, Junior."

"Oh—well—" She picked up the pad, laid it down, then looked at me. For a moment we just stared at each other, with no idea what to say next.

Finally I thought of something. "Can you call him in Washington? I'd like to talk to him."

She nodded hastily and turned to a little rotary file.

I stood back and looked around. The walls were paneled in some dark, lustrous wood. There were long, narrow windows all around, and through them you could see the red and brown bindings of law tomes in the shelves of offices on the other side of the wall. Beside each window hung a framed portrait of a former partner: stern, hirsute Victorian faces, crisp profiles from the twenties and thirties. The receptionist sat at a round black marble counter, its line nicely repeated in the curve of the black marble banister running down the short staircase directly behind her. The only tacky note was the soft, insistent Muzak dribbling from unseen speakers.

The receptionist was talking into the phone. "All right, thank you." She hung up and looked at me regretfully.

"Well, he's not at the hotel, Mr.—er, Lavien."

At first I felt reprieved. Then I remembered that I did not have three and a half dollars any more.

"Can I wait in his office until he gets back?"

The idea appalled her. "But—he won't be back until tomorrow."

"You can't stay the night, Arthur. Only lawyers get to spend the night here."

I recognized the voice at once, and for a moment I was too surprised to move. Then I turned, and I was looking directly into her deep-blue eyes.

Claire leaned forward and placed a kiss on my stubbled cheek, watching me warily out of the corner of her eye all the while. I remembered this greeting from the declining days of our romance: she liked to take care of it quickly so that I wouldn't have an excuse to kiss her on the mouth.

She looked at me with a smile for a moment, then turned to the receptionist. "I'll take care of this, Randi."

"Thanks, Claire," said Randi with relief.

"You—uh, you work here?" I asked. I was having great difficulty organizing my words, as if I were trying to speak French.

"Yes," she said, "since I graduated last June."

"That's quite a coincidence."

"Not at all. Your father got me the job."

"Oh," I said.

"I take it you would like to speak to him?"

I nodded.

"We'll go down to his office," she said and moved toward the stairs.

We descended to a dim, quiet corridor, and I followed Claire's slim figure to a dark oak door marked ARTHUR LAVIEN, SR. She opened it, and we stepped into the small outer office. There were several secretaries standing by the filing cabinets, talking. Maitland, Ruthven secretaries seemed to take the mini side of the great mini/maxi-skirt controversy that was sweeping the nation, and with good reason: there wasn't a bad leg in the bunch. No wonder the old lecher had come here. They nodded to Claire and looked at me curiously as we went through the door to the inner sanctum.

We padded across a vast expanse of carpet and eventually came to a desk before the window. It was a beautiful desk, a stretch of dark, mellow wood rimmed with intricate scrollwork. I remembered it from his office in Hartford.

Claire picked up the phone, standing deferentially on the visitor's side of the desk. I went around it and sat in the comfortable leather chair. Out the window to my right I could see the blank, dark towers of the World Trade Center. They seemed to have grown a good deal taller while I had been away.

"My father's not at the hotel in Washington," I said.

She nodded, unfolding a piece of paper. "I know where to reach him," she said. "He's on the Hill."

She meant Capitol Hill, of course.

"Is he trying to get approval of a merger between Ford and GM?"

"Oh, he worked that out last week," she replied with a grin. "Now they're absorbing Chrysler and AMC, the small fry." Claire was always quick to pick up on a joke, and she would carry it on in a measured, emphatic, absolutely deadpan voice. Once I had found this mildly amusing.

"Hello," she said into the phone. "Is Mr. Lavien there? All right. Ask him to call his office, please." She put the phone back and sat in the "client's chair," facing me across the broad desk.

Claire had been quick to adopt the neat, dreary styles of the seventies, and I was relieved to see that they had made her rather less attractive. The thick, gold-brown hair that used to spill magnificently over her shoulders had been guillotined a precise three-quarters of an inch below the chin. She wore a tan turtleneck and a khaki pantsuit, trim and sleek with epaulets and buttoned pockets. She looked like a paratrooper on inspection.

"So," I said. "What do you do around here? You don't have a law degree."

"No, just a standard Radcliffe A.B." Harvard types never let you forget where they went to school.

I did some mental arithmetic. "You graduated in three years then."

She shrugged. "Standard practice among us grinds."

"You were so crazy about Radcliffe, I thought you'd want to stay there as long as you could."

"Oh, I wanted to get out into the real world."

"The real world." I looked about the big, luxurious office. "You were going to tell me about your job."

"Right. I'm a para-legal. There are several of us in the firm, and they really make us work. I'll be filing the rest of the afternoon, then I've got to run off copies of a brief, and then around seven I'm going up to dear old Hartford to pick up some papers from your father's clients. Your father really brought a lot of business with him to the firm. He—" She would have gone on, but something in my look told her I wasn't interested.

"I thought you wanted to go into Legal Aid work."

She nodded quickly and said, "Right." She did that

whenever you brought up an embarrassing question, as if she had foreseen the point and would now move swiftly to meet it.

"I was interested in that, but it's very dreary stuff. Landlord-tenant, divorces. It's very routine law."

"It's not routine for your clients, and somebody's got to help them."

She pretended to consider the objection. "It helps individuals, but it does little to change the system." She looked thoughtfully out at the World Trade Center. Claire's eyes were an unforgettable shade of blue, like a northern lake on a sunny, autumn day. She had a broad face with large, handsome features; and at moments like this, when she was pleased with her line of reasoning, she wore a look of serene rationality, like one of Raphael's philosophers. "I think," she said, "that at this stage I can do good mostly by honing my own skills as a lawyer."

I let her enjoy that for a while and then replied, "So you work as a lackey for the corporate elite."

She looked at me with an ironic smile. "You still talk like that."

"Like what?"

"All that—jargon."

"I still believe the same things I did three years ago. Are we all supposed to become hypocrites now that it's a new decade?"

"Then why have you come back?" she returned at once.

I looked down at my feet. At my rotting socks. She was right, of course. It was three years to the month since I had left Columbia, and all I had to show for it were warrants for my arrest in four states and lice. And in the end the lice had beaten me.

Claire spoke again. Her tone was conciliatory now. "What have you been doing, Arthur?" But she could not contain her amusement with me. "The usual excursions into politics, drugs, and mysticism?"

"Not the last, no. I'm not quite so ridiculous as you think I am."

We looked at each other for a moment, and then the phone rang.

Claire picked it up. "Mr. Lavien's office . . . Mr. Lavien, it's me." She always said that. What confidence. "Um—I called because—well, Arthur's back. Yes, in the office."

She handed me the phone, turned away, and left the room.

"Hello, Dad."

"Hello, Arthur," said the deep, unhurried voice.

For a moment he was silent. I suppose it could have been surprise, but I think it was lack of interest.

"Well, what brings you back to the East?" he asked at last.

I didn't really have an answer for that.

"I need a place to stay," I said simply.

He hesitated, as if he could not understand what that had to do with him.

"Oh, you want to stay at my apartment?"

"Please."

"All right. I'll call the desk and tell them to let you in. It's on First Avenue, just up from the U.N. The address is Eight seventy United Nations Plaza."

He would live in a building like that.

"Thanks," I said.

Silence.

"Is that all?" he asked.

Yes, that was all. I could hear him talking to somebody else—some Washington biggie, no doubt—even as he put the phone down.

I hung up and leaned back in the chair.

"Well," I said aloud to the quiet office, "now I can get my clean clothes. That was relatively painless."

I tend to tell myself things out loud when I don't believe them.

I got up and left the offices of Maitland, Ruthven,

Lavien, and Stewart. I didn't see Claire on the way out.

Those two brief conversations in ALsr's office had finished me, but for a while I did not know it. I remember, though, that as I passed the United Nations park and looked at the new leaves settling like light-green puffed sleeves around the branches of the trees, a curious thought slipped into my mind: more people commit suicide in April than in any other month. I had read that somewhere.

I walked up to the triple-peaked canopy of United Nations Plaza. There was a doorman in a long grey coat, and again I anticipated a major hassle just to get in. But he merely touched his cap and pushed the revolving door around for me. I reminded myself that long hair meant nothing any more; probably the U.N. Plaza was loaded with plastic hippies who looked just like me.

My father had called the desk, and they gave me a key marked 25-B and directed me to the East Tower elevators. I was surprised my father didn't have an elevator of his own.

I walked into the apartment, into the living room. It had been expensively and impersonally decorated. The carpet bore a subtle pattern in shades of blue, the chairs were black leather, the table steel and glass. I walked over to the glass wall. U.N. Plaza was one thirty-story window; the apartments were all on permanent display to the people across the street on Mitchell Place. It was conspicuous consumption at its best, like living in a department store. I waved to the people in the cocktail lounge a few hundred feet of sheer drop away and went looking for some clean clothes.

I looked in the bedroom closet. Of course, my father had left all my clothes in Hartford. Along with most of his, it seemed, for ALsr had gone mod, or mod by senior partner standards anyway. His suits had only two buttons and wide lapels. His ties were wider, too, than before, and among the rep stripes, I spotted a paisley pattern. Very restrained, of course, but still a paisley. His Brooks Brothers button-down shirts were sky-blue and butter-yellow as well as white; a few of them—very few—bore pinstripes. I selected white —one of us had to maintain standards, after all.

I took the shirt and a pair of fresh socks into the bathroom, peeled off my stiff and stinking clothes, and plunged into the tub.

And just two hours later it was all over.

I sat in the big, comfortable chair, looking at the patchwork of pale orange and shadow cast on the East Side skyscrapers by the setting sun, and knew that I was going to die.

It was not a new idea. Like many lonely people, I had thought often and fondly of death. Suicide is a great consolation—it gives you a choice. You say to yourself, "If things get much worse, I can always end it." But you never do.

Tonight I would.

Curiously I had not thought of suicide in the last three years, miserable as I had often been. And so I did not recognize the signs this afternoon.

I had put on my clean clothes and devoured an apple, a bowl of cereal, and several pieces of bread. Then I tried to think what I would do with the rest of the day. First, I thought I would call some of my old friends from Columbia, but I didn't know where they were, and I would be embarrassed to answer their questions. Then, I thought I would go up to the campus and look around. But that meant a walk and a subway ride, and I wasn't really interested in seeing the place again anyway.

Now I began to realize that my mood was souring

and considered going out to score some dope. But that would mean hunting out my old classmate Larry, and I just didn't feel like it.

By five o'clock, even warming up a TV dinner was too much for me.

And I gave up. I slumped in the chair in the darkening room and let depression soak into me.

I thought, I should get out of here. I should paint "west" on a sign and go out to the highway and hold it up. But I had done that before. I had tried running away three years ago.

I had felt, then, that running away was a meaningful thing to do. When I was expelled from Columbia after the '68 rebellion, I had taken off across the country and expected the fascist war machine to come in hot pursuit. I had the timetable all worked out: in September I would lose my deferment and become 1-A. After my Hartford draft board wrote me a few letters and received no answer, they would call ALsr.

"No, he's left college, and I don't know where he is."

"Well, I'm sorry, Mr. Lavien. We'll have to put out a warrant for your son's arrest."

He would allow that this was perfectly legal.

I expected to be in Canada or in jail by Christmas, and settled down to wait in Berkeley.

And the fascists let me down. They never came for me.

"What the hell, Art," a fellow radical had told me. "You must realize that the clowns who run this war machine have their heads up their asses. There are lots of draft dodgers who never get caught. They probably lost your file."

I suppose I should have sent my draft card back to remind them about me. But I didn't. I just drifted slowly from one big university to the next, working at odd jobs, taking courses, hanging around the fringe of the local SDS chapter . . . "The usual excursions into politics and drugs," as Claire had so disdainfully put it.

Claire. Working for the old man now. How different she was, how—I shuddered as I realized it—how *like him* already. Cool, slick, distant, her humanity being slowly smothered by her growing expertise.

I got up and wandered restlessly to the window, trying to despise Claire and, when that failed, trying to pity her. But how could I? She had a full, busy life; she was getting on with what she wanted to do. And I—there was nothing in the world I wanted to do.

A long, empty hour passed, each moment falling like a blow, weakening me more and more. I didn't move, didn't blink, hardly breathed. The past three years came back to me, seeming infinitely more miserable now than when I was living them. Pointless. I was used up long ago, but I had not realized it; I had had to come home for that. I had lost all hope that I could make this country better three years ago. They had beaten me, and I was only waiting for them to come and finish the job.

But when they didn't come, why was I unable to just get on with my life? There were thousands of young people who had been just as committed as I was. What were they doing now?

The smart ones were slowly, painlessly selling out, like Claire.

I wondered why I had found it impossible to do the same. I was no radical, really. I did not believe in blowing things up. When my draft board gave me the chance to get off the hook, I had humbly taken it. I had been born in a big house, been warm, well fed, comfortable all my life. Who was I trying to fool, pretending that I was a rebel, oppressed by the Establishment?

Myself, of course. I did not want to admit that I was just a loser.

I could not bear to go back on the road, nor could I bear to sit in this quiet, luxurious apartment any longer. Presently I got up and went into the study, and saw with relief that my father had kept all of his guns.

3

I was surprised to see the car they had waiting for me downstairs. I expected a twenty-foot-long black Cadillac, but it was the old grey Mercedes that had been my car in high school. The bodywork seemed boxy now, and the steering had grown crochety with age. Claire Cowan often used to sit in the right-hand seat, smiling ironically at me sideways.

Without thinking, I turned north on First Avenue. I didn't want to die in New York, and some curious homing instinct led me north, toward Interstate 95, toward Hartford.

After half an hour, I veered into the right-hand lane to take the next exit, find a place to pull over.

And, of course, I couldn't do it.

The traitorous part of my mind that wanted to keep me alive had set to work on my will as soon as I picked up the gun. It was clever. It did not argue; it simply delved into my imagination and brought up a sound—the sound of a revolver exploding two inches from my ear. My father had taught me to shoot in the basement of our house, and for months I had winced at the heavy, reverberating roar of the gun going off. Presently another image settled in my imagination to accompany the sound: I remembered hammering tent spikes into soft ground. Just like that, the bullet would drive into my brain.

I reached over and screwed the top of the Scotch

bottle off with one hand. I took a long pull, and then another.

I figured that the liquor would set my blood tingling with courage and resolve, but it didn't. Like many New England kids, I had never been allowed so much as a swig of beer in my youth; and when I reached seventeen, I had started smoking dope. Now I was getting drunk alone for the first time and discovering that booze is a depressant.

For a long time I just followed the hood star of the Mercedes down the broad, busy highway. The needle of the gas gauge was creeping closer and closer to "R." At any moment, the red reserve light would go on, and I would be running out of gas. My father always kept a credit card in the glove compartment; but the effort of finding a station, pulling in under the bright lights, and facing another human being was beyond me. And there was no point to it. If I left the highway, I must pull over and pick up the gun. I had no excuse for continuing this useless journey, this useless life.

So I stayed on the highway, and after a while I sank into a kind of stupor, driving along with the bottle in one hand, watching the needle slide imperceptibly to the left. Now I feared the red warning light, not the roar of the gun. I knew I was not going to do it. I had failed, even at suicide.

A sign flashed past: ENTERING CONNECTICUT. Welcome home, I thought.

Just as the needle touched the curve of the "R," a truck ahead of me pulled out into the passing lane, and I saw the Volvo.

I recognized it at once because the lens on the right-hand taillight was missing. It had been knocked out in the course of sanding rust spots on the fender. Four years ago. By me.

Of course, Claire had told me that she was going

to Hartford; she had even told me when she was leaving—and I had started out at almost the same time. Perhaps, subconsciously, I had come looking for her.

The bare bulb began to flash; she was taking the Greenwich exit. The road to Hartford was strewn with Maitland, Ruthven clients, and she was running another errand on the way. I followed her. I had nothing else to do.

I saw the Volvo turn left at the end of the exit ramp, but the light changed, and I had to wait for oncoming traffic. Then I jumped the light and went after her. I did not see the car ahead, so I turned off onto the first side road. I prowled through the dark, quiet lanes for a few minutes and found it.

The Volvo was parked at the side of the road. I stopped across from it and gave it a last look before turning out my headlights. It was one of those old, humpbacked Volvo sedans. The paint, a dismal cocoa color, faded into coats of primer on the bulbous fenders. I had never finished fixing it up.

The car was empty; Claire had gone into the house beyond, a pleasant little colonial with dark shutters. Lights on the first floor and the front porch threw dim white shadows on the front lawn. Any moment now another square of light would show as the front door opened. I would see her slim figure in the khaki pantsuit, talking to a balding shirt-sleeved executive with a drink in his hand. The porch lamps would bring out the gold in her brown hair. They would shake hands, and she would cross the lawn and throw her briefcase into the car, off to Hartford now, tirelessly about my father's business.

I put the Scotch away and picked up the gun. How lucky, to run into Claire! I had spent the worst hour of my life waiting for Claire Cowan; when I was desperate and needing her, she had let me down. It was all coming back now; with pleasure I felt the bitter despair rising within me. I had found the resolve I needed to finish the job.

Suddenly another car swung around the corner and lurched to a stop beside the Volvo. Leaving the engine running, a kid jumped out of the driver's seat and went to Claire's car. He was hunched over something he carried in his arms.

Without thinking I threw open my door and jumped out. He was a tough-looking kid, with long stringy hair and a leather jacket; and some irresistible bourgeois instinct drove me to protect Claire's car.

I didn't realize until I started moving how drunk I was. I seemed to cover the ground so lightly and swiftly.

I came around his car and saw him leaning in the passenger door of the Volvo. The overhead light was on, and I could see some sort of package on the seat, and there was another in his hands.

I stopped. I had thought at first that he was trying to steal the car. But something else entirely was going on here.

As I hesitated a few steps away, he looked up and saw me. His face was hollow-cheeked and sharp-nosed. He dropped the package and brushed the hair from his eyes with one hand while the other slipped below his jacket.

"Better split, man," he said in a neutral voice, hardly louder than the drone of the car's engine.

I stood where I was. There was a flash of metal as his hand swung away from his jacket.

And then I didn't hesitate. I don't know why I did it. Perhaps I wanted him to kill me, take care of the job for me. Perhaps I just didn't want to take any more shit from anybody.

I lunged at him and swung my right arm at his hand. He wasn't expecting a fight from me, and I took him by surprise.

There was a dull thud as the gun in my hand connected with the side of his head. I had forgotten I was carrying it.

He fell against the door and sank slowly to his knees. He was only stunned—he would be at me in a moment. I backed up a step, and my eyes fell on the two packages that lay on the seat of the Volvo. Again without thinking, without hesitation, I grabbed them up and ran for my car.

The starter seemed to grind for an eternity before it caught, and then I put the gears in third instead of first and killed it. By the time I pulled out and headed for the turn, the kid was on his feet. I glanced anxiously in the rear-view mirror and saw him staggering to his car.

I raced the Mercedes down a hill and into a sharp left-hand corner. Scared as I was, I knew my car would be faster through the turns than his, and I had a start. I drove desperately, whipping the car faster and faster through the quiet, winding streets.

I wasn't looking at anything outside the headlight beams, and I was startled when I straightened out of a sharp bend to find a row of red taillights winking at me. Suddenly my lights focused on two old ladies, arm in arm, about to step off a curb. Their shoulders jumped at the squeal of my brakes.

I stopped well short of them, but I knew they would never forgive me anyway. As they passed in front of the car, they turned grim, seamed faces at me. The nearer one shook her finger.

I took a deep breath, lifted the gear lever carefully into first, let in the clutch, and pulled a few feet forward into a parking space. I switched off the engine and took my feet off the pedals. And then I breathed deeply and waited for my heart to ease its pounding.

After a while I looked around me. To the left was a small, square brick building; through its big windows I could see girls in blue coats against a backdrop of shining stainless-steel ovens. They were putting burgers and shakes in paper bags. I had come in the back entrance to a McDonald's.

This was as safe a place as any, and I flipped on the overhead light to take a look at the packages.

They were identical: ordinary brown cardboard boxes, unmarked, the flaps heavily taped. They were the length and width of shoe boxes but about twice as deep. I remembered that running with them to the car, I had been surprised at their lightness.

I knew what I had seen. These packages were a delivery destined for my father. And because I had seen, the messenger boy had pulled a knife on me.

I flipped off the light and started the engine. It would be interesting to have a talk with Claire Cowan, and find out just what kind of errands she was running for ALsr.

It took me ten minutes to find the street again, and another five to build my courage to drive up it. I inched up the hill, leaning forward and peering nervously along my headlight beams. But the kid's car was gone.

So was Claire's.

I pulled into a driveway and turned around. The red reserve light had come on, so I found my way back to the main drag of Greenwich and pulled into a gas station. I left the car, telling the attendant to fill it, and crossed the cement, shimmering blue under the bright fluorescent lights, to a phone booth.

"Maitland, Ruthven."

"Yes. I want to get in touch with Claire Cowan."

"Miss Cowan? I don't believe she's in this evening, sir."

"Could you check if she's left word where she can be reached?" Claire always did this; she believed that she was indispensable.

"One moment, sir." I heard the dry riffle of papers. "Yes, here it is—if anyone needs to reach her they're to call her father's, in Hartford. The number is—"

"I know it," I interrupted. "Thanks."

I hung up and returned to the car, found the credit card and paid. Then I pulled out and headed for Interstate 95. East, and Hartford.

4

I have enjoyed few things in life the way I enjoyed that drive. Once I even reached over, grabbed a box, and shook it—like a six-year-old on Christmas Eve. It did not rattle, though, and it felt awfully light.

It could, of course, contain cash—a lot of it. But on the whole I thought not, and I was in no hurry to open the boxes. They would probably be full of legal papers, which would be meaningless to me.

But not to the Justice Department.

When I was younger, it had seemed extraordinary to me that my father could make so much money pushing papers around. The care he took of those papers seemed an affectation. We never saw them when he brought them home at night—he worked behind closed doors in his study; and when he went to bed, he locked them in the drawers of his desk.

I remembered an evening sometime in my fourteenth year. We were at dinner when a messenger arrived at the front door with a black portfolio. My father had taken it, signed for it, and solemnly borne it to the wall safe in his study.

Only later did I understand that these papers represented millions of dollars to American corporations, and that men like my father had to be very careful which ones they let the Government see.

He was just as discreet about telephone calls. Many times he would pick up the phone, listen a moment, and nod to my mother. She would leave the room and close the doors behind her. Mother bore up patiently under that, but it annoyed her that he would give out only the number of his hotel when he was in Washington. He wanted as few people as possible to know where he went during the day until his job was accomplished.

Suddenly it struck me: today, Claire had known where to reach him.

All the way to New Haven, I constructed scenario after scenario to explain Claire's involvement in this. Finally, as I swung onto 91 and the stretch north to Hartford, I accepted the simplest and most disappointing of them.

But I knew it was the right one. I could picture old ALsr calling her into his office and saying, "Claire, I have to go to Washington tomorrow, and I want you to do something for me. Drive your car out to Greenwich and leave it on So-and-so Street. Go for a walk. When you come back, you'll find two packages in the car—just some legal papers. Bring them back to my office and lock them up. No need to mention this to anyone, of course. Just give me a call to let me know they're safe."

"Yes, Mr. Lavien," Claire would reply. She knew that the law was a terrible inconvenience to Maitland, Ruthven's clients, and they had to go to considerable lengths to get around it. That's what Maitland, Ruthven was for, to show them the way. And what did she care about the consequences of her work? She was only interested in "honing her skills as a lawyer."

I felt sure, too, that Claire *had* taken a walk—that she had not seen the fight between the kid and me. It had been brief and silent, after all. When she called ALsr, she would not be able to tell him what had become of his packages.

He had gotten the call by now. I pictured him standing in the hall of some mansion in Chevy Chase, gripping the receiver and staring into a gilded mirror at his own disbelieving face as the awesome consequences took shape before him: a multimillion-dollar merger threatened . . . Maitland, Ruthven's reputation endangered . . . corporate biggies facing serious embarrassment, heavy fines, even criminal charges, if those papers fell into the wrong hands.

They had fallen into the wrong hands, all right.

The Cowans' house stood on a hill. The dark lawn rolled up to it like an ocean wave and broke against its blue-white sides in a golden spray of forsythia bushes. The house itself was typically West Hartford—clapboard, square, and tidy, with two symmetrical rows of shuttered windows and a shallow pedimented doorway lit by brass coach lamps.

I left my car on the street and climbed the hill until I could see the driveway. The cocoa-colored Volvo wasn't there.

Claire had told the office that she was going to visit her father, and Claire always carried out her plans. Probably I had gotten here before her.

So much the better. She would find me here when she walked in, fresh from a nervous drive and a harrowing talk with ALsr. I had never seen Claire upset; I was looking forward to it.

The front door opened, and I saw a stocky, broad-shouldered silhouette against the bright hall. Tom Cowan.

"Jim?" he called.

I had no idea who Jim was, but naturally Tom did not expect me. I veered over into the light thrown by the porch lamps.

"It's Arthur Lavien," I said a little nervously.

There was a moment's pause as he peered out at me, and then he said, "Well, good gracious, Arthur!" Tom had come up from North Carolina a decade ago, and he still used expressions like "good gracious."

"Come on in," he said as I reached the door, smiling

and reaching out his hand. It was the warmest welcome I had gotten that day.

"Glad to see you, Tom," I said as I stepped in, and meant it. It is rather unusual to call your girlfriend's father by his first name, but I had always done so with Tom. He had never adjusted to the stiff, frenetic tone of life in the Northeast; he found formality chafing and uncomfortable, like a necktie on a hot summer's day, and he loosened it up as soon as possible.

He had changed little in three years: his sideburns were fuller and greyer, and his hairline had eroded more. His face was broad and strong-featured, like Claire's, and he had the same level, wide-apart eyes. But Tom's were dark and deeply set, and always looked mournful.

"Come on in the kitchen and have a beer." He already had a chilled golden glass in his left hand.

He turned and led the way down the hall, and added over his shoulder, "Claire's upstairs making a phone call."

So, I thought, while I was hurrying around Greenwich, Claire had returned to her car and driven—driven where?

"Claire?" I said, with an attempt at casualness. "I didn't see her car outside."

"She always takes the train and writes it off to your dad. Did you know she got a job from him?"

"Yes," I said absently. I had forgotten there were still trains in this part of the country. Claire, sticking to her routine, had calmly dropped her car at the Greenwich station, and she was only getting around to calling ALsr now.

As Tom swung open the wide avocado-green door of the refrigerator and reached in for a beer, I began to understand that I was making too much of this meeting in Greenwich—or rather, expecting Claire to make more of it than she really was. These clandestine deliveries were probably nothing new at Maitland, Ruthven, and naturally they were subject to scheduling errors and nervousness. Right now, I knew, Claire was saying to ALsr, "Well, he didn't show."

"Really?" would be the reply. "Well, thanks anyway. Sorry to have sent you out there for nothing."

No, the old man would not be worried . . . that is, until he got a call from the frightened employers of the kid with the knife.

With a cold bottle of Michelob in my hand, I followed Tom into the living room. It was a splendid place. Tom's wife had thought, once, that she could make Hartford more bearable by spending a fortune on furnishing her house. For this room she had bought a beautiful Persian rug in a rich, intricate pattern of warm colors and selected everything else to complement it: wooden tables with a mellow reddish tint, easy chairs in brown leather, a pumpkin-colored sofa, and brass lamps and ashtrays. She had even bought a twenty-four-volume encyclopedia because she liked its red and tan bindings.

As we sat down, Tom was telling me a story about going to visit Claire at her office in the city. He had taken the train and ridden beside a man who commuted to Wall Street from Milford every day. As he described the man, his Southern drawl grew rich with incredulity. "Ah couldn' believe it. This pore fellah spent six hours on trains every day of his life. 'Course I didn' blame him. That city—it's an *awful* place." He fixed me with his sad eyes and asked me how I thought Claire could stand it.

It never occurred to him to ask what I was doing there. Tom Cowan was so easy to be with—like a big dog or a good-natured child. He demanded nothing from you, was never uneasy or unduly curious. If he enjoyed your company, he was glad to see you, and he did not concern himself with your motives or problems.

When I had first gotten to know him, I had thought

that this restful indifference was a characteristic of the rural society of the South. But it was unique to Tom. He just didn't put a great deal of effort into his relations with other people. He was a surgeon, and he had told me once that he never "really felt alive 'cepting when I'm up to my wrists in some pore fellah's gastrointestinal tract." He had the medical profession's gruesome sense of humor.

That remark had struck me. Tom's nervous system was geared to the operating room—when a normal person would be nervous and uncertain, he had to be calm. And, naturally enough, when a normal person would be calm, he was half asleep.

He was an excellent surgeon, too. He had been one of the many specialists called in on my mother's case four years ago. "Dr. Cowan did everything that was humanly possible," an internist had told me gently, afterwards. I knew that; I thought he had done too much. It was cancer of the stomach, and we all knew there was only one way it could end. The only question was the cost in suffering.

That was how I had met him—and Claire. I remembered my mother beaming after Claire as she left the hospital room and leaning over to me to whisper, "This illness is a blessing in disguise!" Typically, she thought her suffering was justified because it had brought me together with this glorious girl.

You were wrong, Mom, I thought. Claire was a curse in disguise. And suddenly I remembered something and felt cold inside.

"Tom," I said, "just now, out on the lawn, you called, 'Jim—'"

Tom looked away uncomfortably. "I thought you were Jim Siegel."

"You were expecting him?"

"He's an intern at Wentworth this year. Did you know that?"

My heart was thrashing like a hooked trout, and I

wished Tom would get it over with. But he didn't
like to say unpleasant things to people.

"You were expecting him?" I said again.

Tom swallowed, and now he looked at me. "I
thought he might be going down to the city with
Claire tonight. He has a couple of days off, and—"

"—they're going to spend them together." I stared
down at the bottle in my hands. My voice sounded
very tired. "It's like that, is it?"

"Sorry, Arthur. They've been going together for a
few months now."

"Only a few months? What took him so long?" I
was surprised at the bitterness of my tone and wished
I hadn't said anything.

The telephone in the study rang, and Tom got up
to answer it. I was relieved; I really did not want to
hear any more about this.

It was no surprise. Wimpy Jim was a few years
older than Claire and me, but he had been hanging
around her since our senior year in high school. Waiting for me to burn out, I suppose.

He was a nice enough fellow—he had been at Harvard Med during the '68 strike and worn a green arm-
band—amnesty for striking students. That was as far
as he would go. He used to say things like, "Of course,
I'm against the war, but I don't see how disrupting
the universities will end it." And he had been right,
as it turned out.

I was sure he and Claire were very happy together.
With a conscious effort, I shrugged my shoulders and
turned my attention to what Tom was saying on the
phone.

It was a call from the hospital, and his tone had
taken on brisk authority.

"Pupils dilated and unresponsive? Mm-hmm. Looks
like the Mannitol isn't going to take hold." He was
silent a moment, listening. Then he shrugged heavily.

"O.K. Discontinue resuscitation and get hold of Dr. Stein."

I knew enough medical talk to figure out that Tom had just lost a patient, and I looked up as he returned to the room.

"Lost one?" I asked.

He nodded. "Another couple of kidneys for Dr. Stein."

"What?"

"Some damn fool fell off his motorcycle goin' forty miles an hour. Brain trauma." He explained to me something about swelling of the brain. "But his kidneys weren't damaged. That's why Dr. Stein smiles every time he sees one of those motorcycles—another couple of kidneys he can use."

Tom was like most doctors—he saw a person only as an assembly of organs that either could be made to work or couldn't. This one couldn't and would be broken down for parts.

While he was up, he had fetched another couple of beers—a guest's glass was never empty at Tom's—and now he laid them on the table and settled on the pumpkin sofa.

"Did you see ole Tricky on TV a couple of nights ago?" he asked.

Tom was an old-line Southern Democrat, and Nixon would always be "Tricky" to him.

"No," I answered. I had been sleeping in a bus station in Ohio that night.

"It was another of his 'peace with honor' performances. That man is devious." He drawled out the word contemptuously: "de-vi-ous."

"What did he say?"

"He had some good news and some bad news. The good news is that he's going to withdraw some more troops, eventually. The bad news is he's invading Laos."

He leaned forward and looked at me slyly. "You know, I think all the men he's withdrawing from Viet Nam are endin' up in Cambodia and Laos."

I nodded; I had heard that theory. Perhaps I might get a chance to defy my draft board after all.

Tom sighed and leaned back. "He's goin' to run this country into the ground yet." Again the dark eyes fell on me. "What have you been doin' all these years, Arthur? We were counting on you young people to save us."

Tom had been a university professor for many years, and even though he was now a rich doctor, the required conservative Republican views had never taken hold in him. I remembered talking to him long into the night once, then turning to Claire to say, "Like— your dad's really got his head screwed on right!" That was four years ago.

"Oh," I said, "I've marched miles and painted signs and worked mimeograph machines for hours on end. I even took over the megaphone once when the strike committee got desperate. But in the end, Dick wasn't very impressed with us." I stopped; my voice sounded ragged with fatigue and depression.

But Tom was not overly sensitive to others' sufferings. He only nodded and reached for a little brass box on the table between us. He took out a couple of cigars, and I accepted one.

"You know," he said as he gave me the matches, "I was thinkin' the other day, that ole bastard really will stick around for five more years. He's smart. An' then we'll have Agnew for eight years."

I agreed with that, and Tom shook his head sadly.

"This country's in powerful bad shape."

I agreed with that, too; and then I asked him, "If you think so, why don't you try to do something about it?"

Most people become very uncomfortable when you

ask them that question, but Tom only grinned slyly at
me and took a pull on his cigar.

"You know, Arthur, I've stopped worrying about it.
I know Tricky's in there for good, I know that war
in Viet Nam is never goin' to end. But it just don't
bother me any more."

He nodded solemnly, as if this were the only vic-
tory worth winning.

"You see, I've come to realize that ninety-nine and
one-half percent of the people in this world are a lot
worse off than I am. I've got a safe, warm home and
plenty of money; and most important, I'm a professional man. This inflation don't bother me 'cause the
price of my services just goes up with it. And I'm not
in business tryin' to sell frisbees or some damn fool
thing. People are always goin' to need what I got to
sell. So, I figure whatever terrible things are goin' to
happen to this country, I'll be the last person they
happen to. An' until then, I'm not about to worry."

Once that declaration would have put me in a rage,
but right now it sounded sensible enough. Tom took
a pull on his cigar and leaned close to me.

"But if you young folk start a revolution, I could
surely understand you. Yes, sir, I surely could." He
grinned. "Besides, you'll need doctors just like anyone else."

Tom obviously had not been listening to me, and
I was about to tell him again when Claire did it for
me.

"I think Arthur's out of the revolution biz, Dad."

She walked over and sat down across from me in
an armchair of rich brown leather. It suited her tan
clothes and gold-brown hair. She was smiling broadly.

Well, hello, I thought. Give me a cigar and a couple
of beers, and I forget what I'm doing. Now I remembered that there were two curious packages in the
back of my car. I grinned at Claire.

"True," I said. "I won't be giving the corporate power elite any more trouble."

Like hell I wouldn't. I felt my spirits rising—I had been right. Claire was leaning back in her chair looking at me quizzically, as if she wondered what I was doing here but wasn't really very interested. She had not seen me on that street in Greenwich.

She was talking to Tom now, gossiping about various people at the hospital. When he mentioned Wimpy, she gave me an uneasy, sidelong glance. My look must have told her that I knew, and she quickly turned back and started to joke with her father, asking if Wimpy was setting medical science back twenty years, if he had killed an even dozen patients yet. If Wimpy had been there, he would have joined in. That's the kind of guy he was.

It bothered me to see Claire so much at ease, but of course I could not mention the packages now. I tried to think of a subject that would embarrass her.

There was a book on the table, a new best seller by some Australian feminist entitled *The Female Eunuch.* I knew whom it would belong to—Tom's wife was not very liberated, but she liked to read the stuff to get herself up for arguments with Tom. I waited until the joke about Wimpy ran out, and then I spoke up.

"How's Jean, Tom? Any better?"

Claire looked down hastily at her hands. Tom gave a sigh.

"That poor little woman," he said. "She's gone back to Chapel Hill for a while, and I hope it does her good."

From our earliest acquaintance, Tom had shared with me the misery and guilt his wife caused him. It was not a mark of special intimacy; Tom innocently believed that his problems were of great concern to everyone, and he was always glad to talk about them.

Of course, he embarrassed Claire—capable, self-contained Claire—no end.

I knew the whole story: Tom had been a professor of medicine at the University of North Carolina—poor but, he always said, blissfully happy. Then, ten years ago, he had made the mistake of accepting a lucrative partnership in private practice and come to search for gold in chilly New England. His wife had never been able to start anew in our cold, dull little city. "Everybody in this town is an insurance man!" she had told me once, bitterly.

"Gone back to Chapel Hill?" I prompted Tom.

"Yeah. She just goes down a week or so every month to see our old friends."

Claire sat rigidly, looking down.

"You must spend a lot on air fare," I said. There was no need to be discreet and tactful with Tom; he wouldn't have noticed it.

"She's worth every penny," he answered. "Everything I have, I owe to her." Again he told us how she had worked as a typist to support him all through medical school and his internship.

"She was happy in Chapel Hill, and I had everything a man could want. But then I had to drag her up here, like a blamed fool. She told me it was a mistake, but I didn't believe her. And she was right, as always. We've never been happy here."

All this was only what Jean had told him recently. Claire remembered those last days in Chapel Hill, when she was twelve years old, very well. Her mother had been excited about the move then, talking constantly of their big new house and all the fine things they would now be able to afford.

It wasn't true, either, that Tom was never happy in Hartford. He had risen to the post of Chief of Surgery at Wentworth Memorial, the best hospital in the state; and if you talked to him at work, he would tell you he was the most satisfied man alive.

Often Claire had talked to me about these things, sitting on the pumpkin sofa and leaning against my shoulder. Cool, determined, and rational, Claire could never understand why her parents did not work out the truth about their past and accept their responsibilities.

But Tom was not a responsible man, and he gave all his attention to medicine. When his wife accused him of blighting her life, he surrendered to her bitterness. Then he would get a call from Wentworth and forget about her. It would take sustained effort and concentration to work at the painful problems of his marriage, and they were beyond him.

Of course, his vacillations only served to frustrate Jean Cowan all the more. She was a small, dry woman with bitter lines about her mouth; she looked, as she felt, out of place beside the fine figures of her husband and her daughter. I remembered harrowing moments in this house when Tom was not in the mood to listen to her, and she turned to me for a more satisfactory response; I would nod and mumble helplessly until Claire rescued me.

Now Claire sat immobile and inexpressive, like a person waiting for a train, as Tom went on. He was in one of his low moods, blaming himself for everything. There were really only two things he could do: get a divorce or move back to Chapel Hill. But right now he was too miserable to think about them. Presently the mood would burn out, and he would return to the direct, final world of surgery, where he was at home.

I looked at him, at the dark, deep-set eyes staring at nothing. He took a shuddering breath and spoke.

"She's a good woman, a smart woman. The only mistake she ever made was marrying me. I'm just a selfish bastard, and there's nothin' I can do about it."

Like Claire, I looked down. There was nothing you could say to Tom; you couldn't convince him it wasn't true, and you couldn't persuade him to do anything about it. I know. Both Claire and I had tried. I felt ashamed of bringing up the subject, of using him this way.

There was silence for a moment. Then Claire stood up.

"I'd better go, Dad. My train leaves in half an hour."

For a moment Tom sat as if he had not heard. Then he glanced at his watch and said, "Good gracious, we'd better hurry!" He rose and stepped over to me, stretching out a hand. "Glad to see you, Arthur. Come again."

We shook hands and he left the room.

I turned to look at Claire, but she had already gone into the hall. Once she would have come over to me and said, "I wish you wouldn't talk about that, Arthur. It doesn't do him any good." Now she didn't care that much about me.

I shook off Tom Cowan and his problems, and followed Claire. I had to talk to her before ALsr reached her and gave her the news about the packages. I had to take her by surprise.

She was standing on the front porch, her black briefcase under her arm. I stepped outside and shut the door behind me. She didn't look around.

We were standing by the blooming forsythia bushes. They gave an impression of spring, a false impression. The night was silent but for a rushing wind that rocked the trees around us, their bare limbs showing black against a dirty-grey sky. It was going to rain.

I looked at my car down the road. I wanted to maneuver Claire over there and show her the packages.

"I can give you a ride to the station," I said. "As a matter of fact, I can give you a ride all the way to the city."

"Oh, no thanks. I prefer the train."

"How ecological of you."

She smiled at my naïveté. "Yes, it certainly is ecological," she said ironically. "Also, I can get some work
done on the train."

It was time to start her worrying a little.

"You've already put in a full night, haven't you?
Seeing all those clients in Greenwich."

She didn't flinch. "Greenwich? No, I came straight
up here."

"Oh." I moved a bit forward to get a clear view of
her face. "I'm driving down to the city regardless, so
the hydrocarbon situation will be the same. You might
as well come."

She shook her head, not looking at me. "Thanks
anyway, Arthur."

She was becoming apprehensive now but concealing
it well. I would have to push a little harder.

"So you haven't used a car at all tonight?"

She hesitated a moment now, her mind racing. "I
don't think my car would survive another trip to Hartford."

"It's still that old Volvo, isn't it?"

Realizing she had made a misstep, she turned away
from me. "Yes," she said at last.

I waited a beat, then sprung it. I did not bother to
sound casual. "You see, that's why I thought you'd
been in Greenwich. I saw your car there around eight.
Parked by the side of the road."

She turned now and gave me an openly calculating
look: Did he see anything else? Could he have frightened the messenger away?

At last she turned away again and spoke. She did
not try to sound casual either. "That's impossible. My
car is parked outside my apartment in Manhattan. You
must have seen one like it."

It wasn't a very good answer, but it was the only
one she had. I waited a while to let her worry, then
added mildly, "That's quite a coincidence. There aren't
many of those old Volvos still on the road."

She was staring at the empty driveway, hoping her father would bring the car around soon.

"Yes, it's been a good car," she said absurdly.

I stepped off the porch. This was the moment; she would have to come with me, find out what I knew.

"You're sure I can't give you a ride?"

She turned and looked at me coldly.

"No," she said. "I'd really rather not ride with you, Arthur, frankly."

Tom's station wagon drew out to the side of the house and stopped. Claire turned and walked quickly over to it.

Furious, I turned away.

I went and sat in the car, and watched Cowan's car back out and pass me, going east.

She could not have made it clearer. "I'm not impressed with you, Arthur. Whatever you know, you don't worry me."

Claire would do many things for my father, but she would not subject herself to a rather unpleasant car journey with me. She had a clear sense of her own equilibrium, and she would sacrifice anything to maintain it.

There in the dark I suddenly remembered one weekend toward the end of our romance. I had gone up to Cambridge—solely to have breakfast with Claire, as it turned out. The rest of the morning she had to spend in the library; in the afternoon there were classes; and in the evening she went over to the *Crimson* to play newspaper.

I curled up on the couch in her suite and went to sleep, listening to the music from a party across the Quad.

In the morning she came in, wearing her blue terry-cloth bathrobe. She, naturally, had slept in her bed. Whatever I saw in Claire in those days, it was not easy sex.

I sat up, wincing as the blood fought its way back into my numb left arm. She took the chair opposite me, frowning.

I asked her what we were going to do that day.

"Arthur, I think I'm ready for you to leave now," she announced.

"What?"

She shrugged. "I'm ready for you to leave. I've got a paper due tomorrow, and I can't work as well when you're here."

Apparently I distracted her, when she gave me any thought.

I gave the ignition key a furious twist, and before I knew it I was turning around in Cowan's drive and heading east, toward Prospect Street and Hartford. I have to give myself this much: I know how to get depressed.

I parked on Scarborough Street and got out to look at my house.

It was easy to see. The neighborhood had declined a lot, and there were brilliant streetlights.

But once it had been the best street in Hartford—when white people still lived in Hartford—and the houses would stand until the next highway came through. Ours was enormous and rather grand: stout chimneys and dormered windows crowned the high, steeply sloping roof; and three stories below, a series of columns raised a lintel over a front porch the size of a squash court. The double doors were eight feet wide and topped by an elegant fanlight.

My mother had been particularly pleased with the fanlight. The Lavien family had never numbered more than three, and yet we had lived in this enormous house all my life because my mother liked it. Even as the blacks and Puerto Ricans closed in, and all our friends fled to West Hartford, we stayed. And it was still ours now, though I was gone and my father lived in

New York and my mother was dead. It had outlasted the family, and it looked forlorn. I walked up the long sidewalk.

The house was completely dark, and I feared as I approached it that I would find broken windows and beer cans and piss stains on the porch. But it looked all right. I remembered that Scarborough Street itself was still prosperous and well patrolled by the cops.

Not well enough, though. As I put my foot on the first step, I saw that some punk had scrawled an obscenity on it. I drew my shoe raspingly across the stone, trying to erase it. No luck; it had been done with a spray can. I went on up to the doors.

I peered in through the fanlight and could just make out a few of the black and white squares of the hall floor. There was a broad, beautifully worked old table in the center of the hall, but I couldn't see it.

I always felt a little guilty for caring about this place so much. Wasn't I a socialist? Wasn't I working for an America where people wouldn't live like this? But all that was in the past, and I wanted to know that the house was all right, because my mother had loved it. It had made her think her life was a success.

I remembered early evenings when I was in my teens. We used to sit in the kitchen, my mother reminiscing as she cooked, about the heroic era of her life when she worked as a teacher to support old ALsr through law school. She would work until five thirty, and then hurry home to their dreary apartment in New Haven to have dinner ready for him when he returned from classes. They ate early so that he would have the evening to study. "Those were hard days," she would say fondly.

Even then I wondered what she thought she had accomplished since that time. I could not see that anything had changed except that now he seldom got home for dinner. My father had mastered the law, and he didn't want to be bothered with the more ambiguous or tiresome areas of living. She figured out the bills, ran the house: my father did not even know where the toilet paper was kept. When he wanted to talk to someone on the phone, she found the number, dialed, and secured the person he wanted. ALsr liked to avoid unnecessary human contact. And she raised the son, too, of course. That's why I was never so hot at baseball.

At last I came to understand what made her satisfied with her life: she had the house. It was proof that he loved her.

Mercifully, she did not know she was leaving it for the last time when we took her to the hospital. The doctors knew, but she didn't.

I suppose she had accepted her husband's lack of interest in life, so she was not surprised at the way he acted when she was dying. In the early months, he handled the stoic calm routine perfectly; but toward the end, he could not face waiting around in hospital corridors until they brought her up from radiation therapy, or holding the basin when she vomited. I had to do that.

I remembered visiting her on a brilliant Saturday in May during one of the cancer's brief respites. She had never been a beautiful woman; and now she was thin and pale, and the radiation treatments had caused her to lose a lot of her hair. Her skin looked green against the white pillows. I wanted to run out of the room, but she greeted me with the smile that had consoled and protected me all my life, and I sat down.

We talked about school, about which college I would choose. (I picked Columbia because ALsr had gone to Princeton.) It all seemed as remote to me then as it must have to her. And then she asked, "Where's your father today?"

"He had to go to Washington." He was in Washington, but he didn't have to be there.

She smiled and leaned a little toward me. "I think he's doing so well, to keep on going despite all this."

I managed not to say anything except to assure her, when she asked, that I would do whatever I could to help him. I kept my head down and left soon. She thought he was courageous when he was simply unfeeling. She could veil any action of this strange, cold man. I couldn't.

A spotlight swept the dark porch and focused on me. I looked around and saw a police car on the street. I turned and went down the steps. It was time to get out of here anyway.

There was a beefy arm in a blue sleeve draped over the sill of the car door. "Lookin' for something, buddy?" asked a voice from the darkness inside the car.

I thought of telling him I lived in this house but decided it wasn't worth it. "No," I mumbled and went to my car. When the cop saw it was a Mercedes, he drove on.

I sat in the car and decided there was no point in blaming Claire. My father always found somebody else to do his unpleasant jobs. She was only the latest patsy. Suddenly I wanted to see those legal papers that were worth stabbing me for. I got out and went around the car to the trunk, fetched the packages, and returned to the driver's seat, flipping on the light.

There was a knife in the glove compartment, and I slit the heavy tape and pulled back the flaps.

But the box did not contain papers.

It was stuffed to the brim with thousands of shiny blue capsules. I knew my pills as well as any head, and I ran through the pharmaceutical rainbow. They were light blue—"blue heavens"—Amytal. Downers.

I closed the flaps, picked up the second package, and slit it open. This one contained a lot of stuffing paper, and I dug into it and came up with five little plastic bags. They were full of white powder. Heroin.

I put the package aside and remembered ALsr coming into my room once, sniffing suspiciously for traces of grass. And I laughed.

"All right, you old bastard," I said aloud. "Now I've got you by the balls."

5

Sometime after 1 A.M. I parked on a nearby deserted
East Forty-second Street and went into Grand Central
Station.

A few weary travelers and bums slumped tiredly
or lay fast asleep on the wooden benches. I went to
the rows of dull metal lockers, looking for one with a
key in it.

There was not a single empty one. Bending nervously over the two boxes in my arms, I hurried under the
clock and into the main concourse. All the garish ad-
vertisements—Kool's waterfall and Kodak's slide show
—were turned off, and the lofty, gloomy old place was
allowed a little dignity until the next morning. I
walked along the walls, which here, too, were lined
with lockers, until I found an empty one. I knelt and
shoved the boxes into it, inserted a quarter in the slot,
and took the key.

I returned to the car, feeling a lot better. I did not
want to have the boxes with me when I faced ALsr in
the morning.

By now Claire had called Washington. "Remember
that delivery that went wrong, Mr. Lavien? Well,
something funny's happened. Arthur drove up to my
house in Hartford tonight, and he said he'd seen my
car in Greenwich. He acted very arch and unpleasant
—well, you know Arthur. Now I thought that just
possibly . . ."

He would be sure at once that I had the stuff. It was

too terrible not to be true. And the nightmare would begin for the old bastard.

He would catch the first plane back in the morning and come directly to see me. I looked forward to that interview. I was curious to know what a respectable Wall Street law firm was doing on the receiving end of a drug drop; but more than that, I wanted to see him try to justify himself to me, plead with me to give the boxes back. Yes, I looked forward to that.

As I turned onto First Avenue, the waiting storm broke at last, and broke hard. The rain seemed not to fall but to sweep along the broad, empty street in grey drifting clouds.

I pulled into United Nations Plaza, shoved the gun under my coat, and stepped out of the car. Stinging drops of rain hit my shoulders and back, and I dashed for the canopy.

Before I had even got around the car, one of the twill-coated serfs appeared and swept an umbrella over my head. "Take it, sir," he called above the clatter of the rain on the pavement. "I'll put your car in the garage."

As the elevator hummed deferentially up to the twenty-fifth floor, I stopped thinking. My brain had been racing for five hours, spinning out theories, teasing bitter memories out of their hiding places. Once you start, you can't help going home again.

Now I leaned the back of my head against the paneled wall and my brain shut down. At once my appetites, realizing that I was still alive and they weren't out of a job yet, set to work, urging me to eat and sleep. My stomach felt light and hollow as a Ping-pong ball, while all the rest of my body, particularly the eyelids and knees, had turned to lead.

I trudged into the kitchen—it was bigger than the entire apartment I'd had in Ann Arbor—and up to a shimmering white expanse of refrigerator door. I opened it. As I expected, there were TV dinners stacked like bricks in the deepfreeze. I picked one that promised crisp-fried chicken with creamy mashed potatoes, and put it in the oven.

Then I just stood before the glass door, staring blankly at the shining tinfoil until the dinner was done.

I took it into the big living room, sat down in one of the black leather chairs, and ate, listening to the rain tapping on the dark glass wall beside me. I was munching on the last drumstick when the house intercom buzzed.

I jumped. My nerves were strung tight; I had counted on complete silence until my father's key hit the door later that morning.

There was a little grille by the door in the hall. I pressed a black button.

"Yes?"

"Sorry to bother you, Mr. Lavien." The voice sounded irritated. "There's a man down here who wants to see you."

My heart was thudding against my ribs. "What's his name? What does he want?"

"He says you don't know him, but you've found something of his, and he's come to claim it."

Of course. How naïve I had been to expect my father to condescend to a personal interview with me about this unpleasant matter. He probably had more important things to do in Washington. No doubt this was some underling from Maitland, Ruthven. Perhaps he would explain that my own legal position was precarious. Perhaps he had an attaché case full of money —a bribe.

"All right. Send him up." I released the button.

I went into the living room and turned on a few more lights. Whatever this character tried, it wouldn't work. Finally the old man would have to come to me himself.

The doorbell rang. I stepped into the hall and put the chain up. Then I opened the door.

I found myself looking into the face of a thirtyish man a couple of inches shorter than myself. His dense black hair was closely cropped, but his sideburns reached almost to his earlobes. He had a short, broad-nostriled nose and cheekbones that gave a sheen to his olive skin just below the eyes. Eyes that were pale brown, very wide, and looking at me incuriously.

"You're Lavien."

"Yes."

"You've got the packages."

"Yes."

He nodded, rocked back on his heels.

"Looked inside?"

"Yeah," I said. "I have."

He gave me a careful, appraising look, trying to figure out if I knew what I had seen. After a moment, he gave a shrug, deciding the answer was yes.

"I want to talk to you," he said. "Just talk." And then he did a curious thing: he opened his raincoat and the jacket beneath, and spread them wide. For a moment I failed to understand that he was showing me he didn't have a gun.

I nodded vaguely, shut the door, and hesitated a moment with my hand on the chain. The old man had decided to send a tough guy to scare me into returning the boxes. At first I thought of throwing the double lock on and going to bed, but then I decided he couldn't really do much but talk, and I wanted to hear him out, learn more about this. I slipped the chain and opened up.

He walked past me, looking around the room as he took off his raincoat.

"Not too good, kid. Not too good." The voice was loud and flat. "I coulda had a guy with a piece standin' right beside me. I coulda stepped aside when you closed the door, and when you unlocked it, he'd a been waiting for you."

He carefully folded the coat over his arm. "No, kid, you're not too good."

I walked past him into the living room, grinning to myself. My guess had been exactly right; he was trying to scare me. I decided to put an end to that nonsense right away.

"The desk would have told me if anybody was with you, and nobody can get in this fortress without going past the desk." I sat down facing him in one of the big leather chairs. "And by the way, there are security men patrolling the corridors all night, so I don't think you should try any rough stuff."

He stared at me, and he nodded slowly. He knew what I said was true.

"I told you I just came to talk."

"Fine. Let's talk."

But for a moment he just stood looking around the room—at the thick rug; the sleek, expensive furniture; the lights of the East Side hovering in the dark, rainy night outside the glass wall. He was visibly impressed and silent, and I looked him over.

He dressed like any junior executive who shops at the King's Road boutique of Sears, Roebuck: a bright-blue double-knit sports jacket, a dark-blue shirt, a maroon and white striped tie with matching handkerchief, and slacks in a blue and grey glen plaid. They flared gently over gleaming white shoes. He had enormous silver cuff links and rings on both hands.

His eyes moved slowly around the room, at last coming to settle on me with surprised distaste, as if he were discovering a stain on the carpet.

"How can a hippie creep like you afford a place like this?" he asked indignantly.

I thought for a moment. He came from ALsr, and he must know who owned this apartment. Obviously he asked the question as a screen. I wondered vaguely where my father had found this character, with his cheap, loud clothes and his heavy-handed threats. Did Maitland, Ruthven retain a small crew of enforcers for occasions like this?

I decided to go along with him for a while. "It belongs to my father."

Deep creases appeared at his nostrils, running down to the corners of his mouth. I think that was his smile; he liked my answer. He was impressed with this apartment and glad it didn't actually belong to me.

"Livin' off the old man, huh?" He draped his raincoat over a chair and straightened his damp cuff. "I got a cousin out on the Island. In the scrap metal business, doin' well. Bought a nice home in Great Neck. His kid liked the pad but didn't want to work. So he was livin' at home till he was twenty-five. Dirty kid, long hair. That's all he did all day was grow his hair." Immersed in this narrative, he sat down. He did not feel he had to ask my permission. "For years I kept tellin' my cousin to throw this kid out. Well, finally he took my advice."

He nodded with satisfaction, then looked at me again. "You a college kid?"

"Used to be."

"What college?"

"Colum—"

"One of those punks," he interrupted with a perfunctory nod, as if he had known it all along. "And I'll bet you were one of the hoods broke into the dean's office and got your picture taken smokin' his cigars."

In fact he was right; I had occupied President Kirk's office in April '68. But right now I was tired of exploring the generation gap with this character.

"Look," I said. "You know my name. What's yours?"

He sat back in the chair and looked at me warily. "Tony," he said. "That's enough for you to know."

"O.K., Tony. Let's talk about a couple of cardboard boxes loaded with drugs, shall we?"

Tony got up, paced to the window. He walked like

a short man trying to look tough, putting his weight down hard on the heels, swinging his arms wide of his body like a wrestler seeking a hold. I noticed that the room was slowly filling up with a new smell, and after a moment I placed it: English Leather after shave.

"So what are you plannin' to do with that stuff, kid?"

I was silent; I did not care to answer that one. After a moment he turned back and looked at me. The creases had re-appeared around his mouth; he was smiling again.

"Why, sure. Kids like you, you're always lookin' for new thrills. You want those downers. Maybe you're tired of pot and LSD, want to experiment with the hard shit, too."

And then, finally, I realized who he was. He did not come from Maitland, Ruthven; he represented the other partner in the little transaction I had interrupted. He was the boss of the kid with the knife.

I looked him in the eye and said deliberately. "I'd think you'd be more sympathetic to druggies, Tony. Being a pusher."

Tony did not have normal expressions; his features seemed to operate independently of one another. Now the creases disappeared, the tan eyes blinked a few times. He was uncomfortable.

"You want to go into business for yourself, is that it?" His head nodded contemptuously. "Kids like you, they peddle a few bricks of hash, they think they can handle a big operation."

He looked reflectively out the window; I was in for another anecdote. "There was this kid—a nigger—pushing grass around Columbia. He got pretty good at that; and when he got hold of some hard shit, he thought he could handle it, too. Only the grown-ups didn't like it. They found the nigger bobbing in the Harlem River a week later."

I stifled an urge to laugh. I knew that this had really happened—a man had really been murdered—but Tony's description made it sound like something out of a B-movie.

"Actually," I said, baiting him, "I thought I'd just handle your downers."

He snorted at that. "It takes a long time to build up the distribution network for a pill operation. You, you know nothin' about the territory."

Again I wanted to laugh; the shift from gangster to junior marketing executive was so swift and so complete.

"A rich kid like you," he said. "If you want money, you should ask your old man."

At that I started thinking again. The kid with the knife, Tony's friend, had no idea who I was. There was only one way Tony could have found me: Claire had called my father, and my father had tipped him off.

I watched him carefully; perhaps the old man had also told him to make me an offer for the drugs.

"Tell me more," I said.

But Tony showed no interest at all. He returned to the chair with a shrug.

"About what?" he asked. "If you don't know how to put the touch on your old man by now, I can't help you."

Again he could be covering up. But what good would that do? I knew ALsr was involved. And then, finally, I realized that I must know more than Tony did. ALsr would have as little as possible to do with a cheap hood like this. He had used Claire for the pickup, kept himself out of it. No doubt there was an equally discreet arrangement for the payoff. My father was only a voice on the phone to Tony, and tonight the voice had said, "There will be no payoff until you deliver the goods." He was a smart bastard, old ALsr.

I looked at Tony, crouched in the chair across from

me. He didn't know I was the son of his "client." I was just some rich punk who had gotten in his way. Suddenly I didn't feel like baiting him any more.

"I have no intention of dealing your stuff," I told him.

"Then why are you sitting on it? Look, I'll give you a few bills to return it, O.K.?" He spread his hands affably, but I didn't like his smile.

"I haven't got the packages," I said. "They're in a locker at one of the train stations."

He nodded. "That's O.K. Give me the key."

He was not looking at me; his eyes were measuring the distance between us. I realized the security men in the corridors would do me no good right now, and for a moment I thought of giving him the key. I had thrown a scare into my father, and I still had the knowledge of what he had done—wasn't that enough?

No, I decided, it wasn't.

"No."

Tony stood up very slowly. His weight shifted to the balls of his feet.

"Look, kid. I'm getting that key."

For the first time he spoke softly, and he wasn't funny any more. Instinctively I shrank back in my chair.

"Now this can go one of two ways: you can just give me the key, or you can stand up and take off your clothes, throw 'em over to me, and then lie down on the floor. And you better not move until I tell you."

To my surprise, I felt calm. I knew I was not going to take off my clothes; I was not going to give him the key.

He grinned, took a step forward. He was enjoying this.

"Come on," he said. "You know you haven't got the stuff to stop me. You're a peace freak. You don't want to fight."

He spoke gently, rhythmically. He was trying to

lull me with his voice—at any moment he would jump at me.

I slipped my hand under my coat and took out the gun.

"No," I said. "I don't want to fight. So if you come a step closer, I'll blow your fucking head off."

Tony's smile disappeared. He straightened up, and the clenched hands opened and spread. He had been staring at the gun from the moment it slid from beneath my coat; I did not think he had even heard what I said.

"I don't like guys wavin' pieces at me," he said hoarsely.

"I don't like guys searching me."

"All right," he said, "all right." He backed up a few steps toward the door. "I'm going. Put that away."

Still he watched the gun until it disappeared under my coat again. Then he spoke, his voice even, conciliatory.

"Look, think about it. I don't need the stuff until Friday. I'll pay you five hundred bucks on delivery. That's the most loss I can take on the deal. Now that's the best I can do for you. You haven't got any other choice."

"Don't count on it."

His jaws clenched, but still he spoke softly.

"You're a stupid shithead, Lavien. You shouldn't show a piece and then not use it 'cause you won't get another chance. My deadline is Friday, and I'm gonna have that shipment. And next time it'll be me who has the gun, and I won't mind using it."

"I'm not impressed," I said.

He spun around and went out the door.

I got up, put the chain on, and went into the bedroom.

"Well, Dad," I said aloud. "Your man didn't do badly. Not badly at all." I knew Tony meant what he said. His reaction when he saw the gun had convinced me. Only a man who knows guns, who knows they kill with a tug of one finger, is as afraid of them as Tony had been. Tony used guns; and if necessary, he would use one on me.

I would have been frightened, I would have given him the drugs, if I cared about my life. ALsr had miscalculated. He did not know about the thing that had finally made me stronger than he was.

I have heard that gamblers regard their winnings as "found" money and wager them recklessly. If they lose, they are no worse off than they were when they sat down at the table. I felt that way about the rest of my life. I had been ready to die several hours ago. The rest of my life was a sort of bonus.

I undressed and slipped between the smooth sheets of the double bed. Right now I was protected by a double lock, a steel door, and an army of grey-coated minions. And I would not leave here—tomorrow morning the old bastard would come to me.

After that I didn't care.

I listened to the rain pattering on the glass behind the thick curtains and went to sleep.

6

My subconscious had a treat for me that night. I dreamed of Claire.

I had done so often over the past three years. They were very modest dreams. I simply met her someplace and spoke to her, and she was nice. She made me feel that we might get together again, someday. They were curious dreams because I knew all along they weren't true, and it did not surprise me to wake up and see the roaches crawling across the linoleum floor and realize that Claire was three thousand miles away and, certainly, not thinking about me.

Tonight, though, the dream was especially vivid. I had seen her again and remembered what she looked like. Strange how someone's face fades away from you even if you think of her often.

The dream began with somebody—one of those insubstantial figures who fill the minor roles in dreams—saying that Claire wanted to see me. At once I went looking for her. I don't recall anything about the search except that it seemed to take a long time and I was very excited. Suddenly I saw her, and the background took substance at the same moment. She was lying on a beach by the sea—I suppose I was remembering the Cowans' place on the Cape. She looked up, smiled, and came to embrace me. Not passionately, just as if she was glad to see me. Her shoulders were wet and gritty with sand. As I sat down beside her, I noticed her forearms, tanned dark beneath a light down of blonde hairs. Again I can't remember what we talked about, but I do know she appeared to be at ease with me.

I woke, it seemed, at that moment, and shifted in the sheets. The mood of the dream lingered briefly; and I thought, very clearly, I don't mind the way Claire treated me anywhere near as much as the way she made me treat her. The suspicion in her eyes, the unhappiness whenever she had to see me. Still half asleep, I thought of that last harsh encounter on the Cowans' front porch.

And then I remembered why she had been unhappy to see me last night, what she had done, and it all came back.

I sat up in bed. There was a bright border of sunlight along the bottom of the beige curtains, and I fumbled for the clock: it was past noon. Where *was* the old bastard?

The chain was on the door, and he couldn't get in without waking me, but still I jumped out of bed and went through the apartment, half expecting to find him, frantically searching the cupboards and closets.

The big rooms were empty, though, except for the brilliant light that poured in through the glass walls. It was a fine day, and I felt good as consciousness pushed my reaction to the dream further and further away. A great deal was going to happen today, and I meant to take each moment as it came.

I went back into the bedroom and opened the closet to treat myself again to the luxury of putting on fresh clothes. Running through a rack of ALsr's new two-button suits, I found a pair of old trousers that looked familiar. They were baggy corduroys, the wale worn nearly flat at the seat and knees. They were mine. For a moment I was angry at the old man for taking my clothes.

I put the pants on and went to the dresser. Under a rainbow stack of golf shirts I found one of my old

Lacoste pullovers. It was one of the flaws in my revolutionary image that I always wore shirts like this. With a smile I remembered a picture of me in the *Spectator* the time I upset Princeton's number one singles player. My long hair bound back in scarves and rubber bands, I was nonetheless wearing forty dollars' worth of whites from Lacoste. In those days everything I wore except my jock had an alligator on it.

Claire affected a great disdain for alligator shirts; she said they were "too preppie." That was the pinnacle of her radicalism. I remembered her telling Jim Siegel and me about it once, when we visited him at Harvard. I told her I would stick by my shirt, but Wimpy jumped up, got a stack of them out of his closet, and cut the alligators off with a razor blade. He made a big routine of it, saying that he intended to pass them out to deserving public school kids, and Claire laughed a lot.

Wimpy Jim. He knew the way to go about winning Claire. He was welcome to her.

I went into the kitchen, opened the refrigerator, and marveled at the thick pink slabs of bacon that were all mine. Had I really been hungry twenty-four hours ago?

I ate a big breakfast in the sunny dining room, then lit one of my father's cigars. I had nothing to do until he showed up, so I started to think it all over.

Until now I had not wondered why my father needed two boxes full of drugs. They were such a beautiful present to me; I suppose I feared they would disappear if I questioned them.

I had thought vaguely that they were destined for his office. But I had no real reason to believe this, and it was absurd to suppose that Maitland, Ruthven, Lavien, and Stewart were pushing on the side. I watched the thick blue smoke curl into the sunlight and thought, No, the old man is doing this on his own.

He just used Claire because she was available. The office, I remembered, thought she was in Hartford last night. ALsr had been using a para-legal for personal errands on company time. Shocking.

So he wanted the stuff for himself. Wanted several thousand downers and some baggies full of heroin.

I started calculating. My knowledge of hard drugs was slight, but I figured there was enough heroin in that box to supply an addict in a fairly advanced state —one who needed a shot every six to eight hours—for about two weeks.

Was my father a junkie? I laughed out loud when that popped into my head. So little of life got through to him anyway that he would hardly need reality softened. He had been stoned on law for the last thirty years.

And it was ludicrous to picture him as a dealer. He made at least a hundred and twenty-five grand a year and loved his work so much that he hardly had time to spend it. No summer houses or European vacations for him; he took a week off in the fall to kill ducks, and that was it.

I thought about the pills some more. Amytal was a fast-acting barbiturate, often prescribed as a sleeping pill. But there was a respectable, middle-class black market in them: a lot of upright, uptight citizens had nerves so completely shot that they couldn't get through the day without popping a dozen downers. What else did I know about them? A lot of druggies popped them together with uppers for a new high. What else?

Then I remembered: well-heeled junkies used downers with heroin to intensify their highs, and without it, to keep them going between shots.

ALsr's delivery contained enough downers to keep several addicts going for months, but he had only enough heroin for one.

One junkie. But who? Why would my father do that for anybody?

The intercom buzzed, and again it made me jump. Then I got up and strode angrily to the grille. If this was Tony come to have another talk, I would tell the serfs downstairs to throw him out.

"Yes?"

"Mr. Lavien, there's a young lady here to see you—"

"Fine," I interrupted. "Send her up."

I released the button and sat down. How delightful. This would be Claire, of course. ALsr had called Tony, gotten the surprising news that I was standing firm, and decided it was time for the soft touch. This is your fault, Claire, he had told her. Go and plead with Arthur for those packages. And she had consented. How low Claire had sunk.

The doorbell rang, and I went to open up.

It was not Claire.

She was a very pretty girl of about my own age. She stood in the doorway with her hands in her pockets and smiled timorously at me.

"Arthur?" she asked in an apprehensive voice, as if we were old friends but she was afraid I would not recognize her.

"Yes."

She raised a hand and scratched at her neck. She looked painfully ill at ease. I felt almost sorry for her.

"Can I come in?" She said it as if she expected me to say no.

"Sure," I answered and stepped aside.

She gave me another little smile and anxiously stepped in. I shut the door and walked around to face her.

Her head was down and she was scratching at her neck again. She looked so miserably embarrassed that I felt I had to help her.

"I know what it's about," I said gently.

She looked up at me gratefully and nodded, and then once more she scratched herself and seemed totally at a loss.

"Come and sit down," I said, leading the way into the living room. The incongruity of all this was throwing me off balance; it was like a first date with an extremely shy girl.

I padded across the blue carpet and took a chair. But the girl had stopped in the entranceway and was looking around the room in silent awe, as if she were in the Sistine Chapel.

The young secretary, I thought, seeing the big boss's pad for the first time. I figured she must be from Maitland, Ruthven; she was certainly good-looking enough.

For a while I just sat and stared at her. She was such a perfect all-American beauty: the thick, honey-blonde hair falling straight to her shoulders and spilling heavily over her powder-blue jacket; the broad-cheeked face, guileless and open; the short, turned-up nose; the full-lipped mouth.

But there was something disturbing about her. The skin, which should be tanned from an Easter vacation in Florida, was very pale. And the eyes, wide and light blue under sandy brows, held a curious look, intense yet unfocused.

Again her hand rose and scratched, this time at that admirable nose, and her glance fell on me.

I remembered Tony's reaction. "Do I look out of place here? Too freaky?"

"Oh, no," she said hastily. "It's not that."

"Thanks."

"I mean, you don't look out of place here. You look sort of—sort of preppie." She laughed shyly.

I couldn't help grinning back. "You've got me," I said. "I went to Loomis."

She gave me her real smile now, a beautiful smile,

and came to sit down in a chair across from me.

"I didn't think you guys said that. I thought you always said, 'I was at Windsor.'"

I stopped myself from grinning. We sounded like two coy freshmen at a mixer, and it wouldn't do. I had to be sure where this girl came from, and her last words gave me an idea.

"I suppose Claire Cowan told you that, huh?"

She winced and looked away, and absently gathered her jacket around her. Too late she mumbled, "I don't know anybody named Claire Cowan."

She did, though. She came from Maitland, Ruthven, and no doubt she knew my father, too. The old man had decided to try charm. I wondered what he had told this poor girl to say to me.

I leaned forward and tried to sound firm and matter-of-fact.

"I gather the old man realized it was a mistake, sending Tony?"

The blue eyes gave me an anguished look, and she rose and wandered toward the window. I felt low, as if I were tormenting her unjustly. I looked at her back, at her hunched shoulders.

"I don't know what you're—" she began, then stopped. She turned around, giving up with a sigh. "O.K. It was a mistake sending Tony. I'm sorry. It wasn't my idea."

I nodded. I believed her.

"Was he—was he real hard on you?" Her tone reminded me of my mother asking me about a tough Latin exam I'd taken in high school.

"He suggested he might enjoy killing me if I don't give him the stuff by tomorrow."

She shuddered and came to sit across from me.

"But you didn't give it to him. That's—that's pretty brave."

I shrugged, like a modest football star, and watched

her. Now it was her turn, and I wondered what she would try.

She leaned forward. "I came to ask—" She stopped and scratched, this time at her arm. And then she looked at me with those intense, distant eyes.

"Would you give it—some of it—to me?"

Was that all there was to my father's final try?

"Why should I?"

She looked down and said in a low voice, "Because I need it."

And she scratched at her neck.

I should have guessed from that. Addicts always itch, even when they don't need a shot.

I looked down, too. I had no idea what I should do.

The girl went on. "I'm not really bad—I mean I can still hold a job and everything. But I had this operation a—a few months ago, and it was really bad. They gave me a lot of morphine in post-op; and after I was discharged, the pain was still there. . . ."

I stood, feeling shocked and helpless, and looked down at that lovely blonde head. Of course, I knew that there were thousands of middle-class junkies, but to look at this girl, just my own age, and know that three times a day she tightened a belt around her arm and shot heroin into her veins . . .

And if she did not get her shot, she would be in agony. I had the stuff she needed, the stuff that was slowly killing her.

She looked up at me.

"Please. You don't have to give me all of it." She paused, trying to think of some other way of making her request as small as possible. "Just think about it, O.K.? I don't need it right away. I have enough until tomorrow night."

"I know—Tony told me."

"I'm sorry about that," she said again, looking away.

There was silence for a moment; neither of us knew

what to do. Nervously she tugged off her jacket and let it fall behind her on the chair. Out of lascivious habit I glanced at her white blouse, looking for the pockmarks of her nipples where the cloth rose and tautened. They didn't show; she was wearing a bra.

I felt ashamed, but I couldn't help it. She was very beautiful, and I had been lonely and frustrated for a long time. It was just habit.

And then I realized that she had seen the direction of my glance. I turned away.

"Wait," she said softly, and suddenly there was eagerness and confidence in her tone. "I can stay a couple of hours, if you'd like that."

At first I did not know what she meant, and then I did.

"I—I won't give you the stuff."

"It's all right. I want to stay."

I walked away from her, toward the wall; I had to tug at the crotch of my pants. I felt bad, ashamed, but I wanted her. I listened to the small sounds of her fingers against cloth.

I felt her hand on my shoulder and turned. She was naked to the waist; her slender arms were up, reaching for me, offering herself to me. I embraced her, and her mouth was soft and warm, her body firm and willing, pressed against mine through the thin cotton of my shirt.

After a long moment she laid her head against my shoulder, rocked gently in my arms.

"Come on," she murmured. "Dearest, please."

I tried to tell myself, You are not dear to her; she is doing this because she needs heroin. And it will work. If she stays an hour, she will leave with the key. You will be supplying a junkie. You'll have to because you've slept with her.

And then, finally, I understood, and the shock made me numb.

I dropped my hands, stepped away from her.

"You're his lover. That's why he gets you the shit."

Her hands moved to cover her breasts. She looked at me fearfully, nodded.

I was beginning to shake, and my throat had tightened so that I could hardly breathe.

"Get dressed," I said hoarsely. "Get out. I won't give it to you."

Then I could not face her a moment longer. I spun around and veered blindly into the kitchen like a drunk about to be sick. I did feel sick, and for a long time I stood hanging onto the counter, swaying dizzily.

At last I heard the front door close, but still I did not want to move. Fury and disgust welled up inside me; I hated the girl. She had almost made me as bad as the old man.

Why had she tried to make love to me? She was not desperate yet; she had enough stuff to keep her going another day. . . . Maybe she did it because she enjoyed it; maybe she got a thrill out of seducing her lover's kid, playing the same trick on the son as on the father.

Then I remembered that open face with its large blue eyes, and a few scraps of rationality returned. No, I thought, and then I said it out loud, "No, that isn't fair."

I took a deep breath and let go of the counter, straightening up slowly. I liked this girl, and I had shown her I desired her. She had to have the drugs, and there was no use blaming her. She meant me no harm—exactly the opposite. As long as I had those boxes, my life was in danger. If she had gotten them away from me, I would be safe from Tony. There was no way for her to know that I wasn't interested in my life any more.

I turned and went back into the living room. I remembered the way the girl had looked at it—of course, she had never seen her lover's home before. He had dealt with Joanne, his girl in Hartford, the same way: broken her in on a "business" trip to Bermuda and afterwards gone to her apartment. His sense of propriety was impeccable.

I slumped into my chair and looked at the one the girl had taken. She was far prettier and far younger than Joanne. She did not seem especially intelligent, but he probably liked that, too.

How unpleasant it must have been for him when he realized that she was slowly slipping into drug addiction! There might have even been moments when he couldn't concentrate on the brief he was writing. Human weakness always upset him; he could not understand it.

Certainly he would not take it upon himself to persuade her to seek treatment. That would require a good deal of time and effort, and might involve him in explanations he would not care to make.

He could simply drop her, of course, but that could drive her into bitterness and desperation—no telling what she might do. Besides, she was a honey and he did not want to lose her.

But there was a half-finished brief lying on his desk. He had work to do and could not allow his attention to become debilitated with thinking about this unpleasant problem.

I remembered one evening long ago. He was sitting at the head of the dining room table, sipping his coffee and explaining the fine points of one of his recent successes to my mother. She was a responsive audience, and he became expansive and delivered himself of one of his few broad reflections about life. "You know, the key to anything is to be practical—take the most direct approach to any problem."

If the girl needs drugs, supply her with drugs.

He probably came to like having his mistress so utterly dependent on him. Not that he was a domineering man, but it saved so much valuable time.

He had taken the direct approach to the problem

I posed, too: How will I get my son to cooperate? The same way I got involved, of course. He had called the girl and told her, "My son has gotten hold of your drugs. It's up to you to get them back."

"It didn't work, you old bastard," I said aloud to the empty room. "And now I know everything. When you get here, you're gonna have to do a lot of talking. You'll know all along that it won't do you any good, but you'll have to try it. I've got you."

I turned to the door, wishing he would come in at this moment, when my anger was at its highest pitch. Come on, I thought, what are you going to try on me next? Threats? Cool, legal persuasion? Or will you be deeply wounded, ask how I can do this to my own father?

Do what to my father? The thought fell like a blow, and suddenly I knew, knew for sure, that he was not coming.

Why should he? What threat did I pose to him?

I flung myself out of the chair and paced to the window. I had accomplished nothing. I had given Claire an uneasy moment. Cost a pusher some worry. Earned myself a death threat. And right now I was causing a beautiful young woman, who also happened to be a junkie, agonies of fear.

I had hurt everybody except Arthur Lavien, Sr.

He had not troubled to do more than make a few phone calls, to put the matter in the hands of Tony and this girl. If I didn't bend to threats or promises of sex, I still presented no difficulties to him. When the girl called, he would comfort her and order up some more junk from Tony. He had another day, after all. And he had plenty of money.

There was one thing I could do: go to the police right now. But then I pictured myself walking into the station with the boxes under my arm. What would the pigs think of a long-haired kid bringing them thousands of dollars' worth of drugs and telling them stories of a midnight rendezvous, suspicions of his own father, a distinguished Wall Street lawyer, ally of the powerful?

I must get some proof. But how could I? I had already heard Claire's denial; she would be willing to repeat it in court. And I had no idea where to find Tony or the girl. Not that either of them would help me anyway; they both needed the old man.

For a long time I paced the floor, trying to think of another link in the chain connecting my father and the drugs, somebody I could find and pin down, somebody I could break.

Suddenly I stopped. My thoughts had hit a snag, an unanswered question that had bothered me earlier.

Tony. How had my father gotten in touch with Tony? ALsr never ventured out of the world of corporate law. How had he been able to find a pusher? The only contacts he had ever had with the drug culture were friends of mine.

I smiled sardonically when that occurred to me, and then I thought of Larry Preston and stopped smiling.

When I had left the East, Larry had been busy building a thriving business in dope and acid. Here. In New York.

I ran to the bedroom and grabbed my coat. The one with the key in it. I was going out.

I shut the door and walked down the long hallway to the elevators. The doors slid open as soon as I pressed the button, and I remembered a pet superstition of mine from the old days: if I had to wait for the elevator, I used to turn around and go back to bed. If the elevator was waiting for me, I would have a good day.

I smiled as I stepped in and pressed One. This was the last good day I would ever ask for.

Thirty hours later I was to recall that elevator ride with a sort of astonishment. It was the final moment when I thought I had things under control, a last lucid pause. I felt fine, better than I had in the previous three years. During that time I had been living in the ruins of my pathetic hopes, hopes that I could stop America from killing Asians and wrest it from the grasp of the pigs, hopes that Claire and I could get back together.

Now I was finished with my confused, unhappy life and all its failures. I felt at peace, as if I had really pulled the trigger last night. There was no hope in me and no fear. I wanted only to bring the old bastard down with me.

7

The doorman turned as I came out.

"Good afternoon, sir."

It certainly was: a perfect April afternoon when you can almost feel the sun at work, warming a pure-blue sky, moving closer and bringing back the spring. I took off my jacket and slung it over my shoulder, then headed west.

In the curious hush that hung deferentially about the doorway of United Nations Plaza, I heard a car door slam and looked up. A stocky, middle-aged man in a tan jacket stood beside his car on the slope of Mitchell Place, looking down at me. As I glanced up, he turned quickly and locked his door.

I turned, too, and walked on. I had half expected to see the kid from last night, the one with the knife. But this could be another of Tony's friends, here to keep track of me until the boss returned to settle accounts tomorrow. Or he could be a man who just happened to get out of his car as I left the building. On the whole, I wasn't really worried about it.

Half an hour later, I stepped off the train into the dank, chilly glare of Sheridan Square Station. This station had always reminded me of a bathroom. Something about the white tiled walls. Something about the smell, too. On the steps I turned and looked behind me. There were a lot of people on the platform, and I did not see the man in the tan coat.

I came out into the sunlight and walked for a while through pleasant, little streets lined with narrow old townhouses.

Larry lived west of the Village and north of SoHo in a nameless neighborhood of ancient warehouses, where the air was full of the grind and roar of trucks fighting their way in from the docks and the Holland Tunnel. I turned onto his street, walked past a little row of shops that kept the steel cages on their windows even in daytime, and stepped into his doorway. I had not been there in years, of course, but I could almost recognize it from the smell: lots of drunks stopped off here at night.

I rang the bell several times and got no answer. With Larry, this did not necessarily mean no one was home. I waited patiently.

Larry always claimed that he was the first head at Loomis. Certainly our parents were warning us to stay away from him as early as '66, and the narcs began tapping his phone—or so he claimed, and made us all call him up and listen to the clicking noises on the line.

But he was proudest, I think, of being banned from stately Lavien manor by the old bastard himself in one of his most magnificent scenes. I remembered the episode clearly; it was almost the only time he seemed to take an interest in my life.

"What is that bum going to do when he graduates?" ALsr had asked me. "Lay around the house, I expect."

I told him Larry had been accepted at NYU.

"Majoring in drugs?"

He had been right, that time. And no doubt, he had remembered.

At last the door clicked open. I went in and up the narrow, musty staircase, and knocked on Larry's door.

"Like who is it?" called a muffled voice from inside.

"My name's Arthur—I'm a friend of Larry's."

The door opened a crack, revealing a shaggy face.

A hand pushed the dark, greasy locks back from one bloodshot eye, which appraised me. Then the head pulled back, and the door opened wide. I stepped in.

"Is Larry here?"

He was a sallow, skinny freak; he swayed slightly as he fumbled with the top button of his jeans.

"Like I don't know. I'm just crashing for the night." He got the jeans fastened and straightened up, pushing back his hair.

"Uh—Robbie's here," he added at length.

"O.K. I'll talk to him. Where is he?"

The freak turned unsteadily and pointed with a drooping finger at a closed door. I crossed the room, ducking under the network of wires connecting the stereo speakers. The blinds were shut, holding in all of last night's smoke. Popcorn and a crust of pizza crunched under my feet.

"Robbie?"

A pause, then a sleepy voice said, "What's happening?"

"It's Arthur Lavien, Robbie."

"Oh—hey, Artie—come on in, man."

I pushed the door, and it swung two feet and jammed against something. I slipped through the opening.

The door had hit the end of an enormous waterbed, which stretched away into total darkness. True citizens of the counterculture don't believe in getting up early.

"Hey Arthur," said a voice from the gloomy head of the bed. "Come on around and crack a shade. Is it like a nice day out?"

"Gorgeous," I assured him, feeling my way to the wall and along it. I found the shade and pulled it up.

The light flooded cheerfully in and showed me Robbie's head amid lumpy pillows and tangled sheets. For a moment I thought he had grown his dark hair even longer recently. Then I realized that most of it belonged to a girl nuzzling her head into his shoulder.

The etiquette of this situation demands that the girl keep her face turned away, and the two of you talk as if she weren't there. I know. I have been in this situation many times. On the solitary end, of course.

"Hey, man, glad to see you," said Robbie, stretching a hand up to me. The girl slipped a little further down under the covers.

"How long you been back?"

I pulled up a chair, causing a stack of *National Lampoons* to fall off and slither to the floor. I thought I would feel more at ease sitting down.

He propped himself up on an elbow. "You need a place to crash?"

"No thanks, man."

His hand found its way into the girl's hair, and he stroked it absent-mindedly. I turned away, only to have my eyes fall on the forms of their bodies, pressed together under the sheet. I looked up at the ceiling.

"Actually, I'm looking for Larry."

"Larry doesn't live here any more. He's moved to the goddamn suburbs."

"He's not at NYU any more?"

"He dropped out. He's a lousy capitalist now. Lives on this farm in Putnam County. He only comes down here on business trips. Goddamn commuter."

"A capitalist?"

"Yeah. He's like really into dealing in a big way."

That was what I wanted to hear. My heart was thumping with anticipation.

"Where can I find him?"

"I got his address somewhere." Robbie made an effort to get out of bed, but it was awfully pleasant in there, and he fell back beside the girl.

"It's on the desk. Blue notebook."

I went to the desk and found the book. Larry's house was on one of those state roads east of the Taconic, an hour or so out of town.

"Thanks, Robbie."

"Sure, man. Keep on truckin'." Even freaks didn't say "peace" any more. I left Robbie snuggling back in with his girl and heard her giggle as I shut the door.

I started downstairs, trying to feel really high about finding Larry, but for a moment I could not; my good mood had faltered. . . . The new sexual openness can really depress you if you're not getting laid regularly, and it had been a long time since I had been in that happy state.

During my first months on the road and in Berkeley, I had presented a romantic figure—the gallant, doomed draft resister. Several girls had taken me into their beds, as an act of political solidarity as well as passion. But as time passed and the threat of prison or exile dissipated, my thoughts turned more and more to the past, and to Claire. My imagination became obsessed with a confrontation between us: I would say, how could you neglect me and finally let me down when I needed you most, and she would shrug and tell me she'd been busy lately. I began to lose interest in the girls I was with, and they in me. Soon my memories of the good times with Claire were the only company I had, and my bitterness toward her only sharpened my yearning for them.

Turning over these dismal, pathetic memories, I stepped out on the sidewalk. It was almost a relief to see the stocky man in the tan coat waiting for me. Come on, I told myself, you've got more important things to worry about now. Your lousy life is behind you.

I turned and started walking east on Christopher Street. At the corner of Bleecker, I stopped and waited obediently for the "walk" sign, and glanced over my shoulder. The man in the tan coat was looking with rapt interest at a display of pipes and roach clips in the window of a head shop behind me.

I tried to clear my mind of a fog of old movies and

come up with a plan. There are situations that just cannot seem real, and one of them is being "tailed." I started across Bleecker, figuring that in actual fact it must be very difficult for one man to tail somebody on a crowded street. I should be able to lose him.

And that is what I had to do. If he followed me up to Larry's and reported back to his boss, Tony might decide to forget his deadline and take me out before I got too close.

I turned south on Bleecker, walked to Grove, and turned east. It was just what I was looking for: the short street was loaded with clip-joint head shops, their junk overflowing to stands on the street. There were also a few longhairs sitting on the sidewalks beside blankets strewn with Indian jewelry and brass roach clips. Little eddies of Long Island teenagers stood staring at the merchandise while thin lines of New Yorkers circled around them.

In long, swift strides I plunged in and, weaving back and forth across the pavement, made my way through the crowds to Sheridan Square. Subway steps opened before me, and I went down them, sprinted through the short corridor and came up again on Seventh Avenue.

To my delight an empty cab came bumping along the wide street just as I reached it. I signaled it to stop, jumped in, and told the driver to go to U.N. Plaza. Then I looked back. No tan-coated figure stood at the curb. I had lost him clean.

8

For ten minutes after leaving the state route, I jolted and slid along a winding gravel road, kicking up a wake of drifting white dust behind me. At last I saw a mailbox with L. PRESTON painted on it and turned off onto a narrow, dirt stretch. It was lined with an untidy row of flourishing hedges, and through them I caught glimpses of red clapboard: I was passing the house. The hedges ended abruptly, and I turned in.

There were several cars—all wearing a pall of white dust—parked on a rise of bare, rutted ground. I left mine and started up the hedge-lined driveway.

It was a sturdy, old farmhouse, coarse red clapboard with a steeply pitched grey-slate roof. But the present owner was something of a slob: the shutters had fallen from the large front windows and been left to clutter the spacious wooden porch, and the paint was peeling off the dented drainpipes.

There was no sign of life here, so I walked on. A garage in newer, narrower clapboard had been added to the place, and inside were a big motorcycle and a green VW camper with all the trimmings.

Larry stood with his back to me, looking in the open side door of the VW. A girl with long brown hair stood beside him, her arm around his back, the hand stuck familiarly in the pocket of his jeans.

He turned and saw me, then gave a surprised grin. "Artie! Hey, man, glad to see you!"

He came up and we shook hands, thumbs out. Larry

had soft, rosy cheeks and small brown eyes that girls always insisted had a twinkle in them. Despite his long dark hair and luxuriant beard, he still looked a little babyish. He asked how long I'd been back, and I told him. He asked what I'd been doing the last three years, and I shrugged and said he had a nice house.

"Yeah," he replied. "At least it's out of range of the bad vibes of the city. I hate that place."

I looked in at the VW and the cycle. I had an idea how he had paid for all this, and I hoped he would tell me about it.

"Some nice transport you've got here, too."

He shrugged. "Aw, they're just things." He looked at me solemnly. "And thing's aren't important, y' know. People are what counts, man."

The chick came up and put her hand in his back pocket again. He put his arm around her and introduced us. Her name was Beth, and she was very pretty. On the whole, Larry had an excellent setup here. He stood grinning at me, and his eyes really did twinkle.

He seemed surprised to see me and completely at ease having me here. That meant that neither Tony nor the old man had called to warn him about me. Probably he had forgotten for the moment the little job he had done for ALsr some months ago. That suited me—I would wait for the moment and draw him out slowly. In high school Larry had always been a willing liar but not a courageous one. If a teacher really had the goods on him, he caved in.

And I had the goods on him.

The screen door slammed, and we looked up to see a girl leaning over the wooden rail of the porch.

"Larry?" she called. "Dinner's ready."

He turned to me. "Want to like stay and do up some food, Artie?"

I assured him nothing would please me more, and we walked to the house.

The hallway was dark and musty, and the wooden floor had sagged with the weight of years. We went through into the kitchen.

There were half a dozen people in long hair and jeans, carrying pots and dishes from the stove and cupboards to the big, round table. Larry sat down, putting Beth on his left and me on the right.

"Hey, everybody, like this is a friend of mine from pr—"—he almost said prep school; old habits die hard —"high school. Artie." Then he ran off a string of first names and a half dozen heads looked up and nodded. They were impossible to remember: they all ended in "ie." Larry favored diminutives.

Big dishes of beans, hot dogs, and some seaweedy stuff that must have been spinach were passed around, along with gallon bottles of a California Chablis. For a while he and Beth spoke softly to each other and giggled, then he turned to me.

"So, you been up to Hartford since you got back east?"

"No," I replied at once, not knowing exactly why I chose to lie.

He nodded. "Don't want to see your old man, the Judge? I can like get into that."

I looked away, frowning. Either he didn't know my father had moved to New York, or he was testing me because he had just remembered that I was the son of one of his clients.

"He's not a judge, just a lawyer," I answered, then added offhandedly, "He lives in New York now."

I watched him carefully, expecting him to feign surprise. But he only nodded and smiled. "Is he still as uptight as ever?"

"Yes," I said, and stared down at my beans. How could Larry speak of the old man so casually?

For the first time I allowed myself to think that it

was possible—even likely—that ALsr had contacted Tony through somebody else. But if Larry was not involved, what would I do now?

Miserably I reached for the wineglass and drained it, and then the fog lifted from my brain.

Dummy, I told myself, even Tony doesn't know whom he's dealing with. Of course the wily old bastard wouldn't have contacted Larry himself—he would have sent the girl down. It was her problem, after all.

I looked sideways at Larry, who was wiping catsup from his beard under the direction of Beth, and imagined the scene when the girl came to see him.

"I've heard you can help me—or maybe you know someone who can." And she told him her problem.

"Like who sent you?" There would be suspicion in Larry's twinkling little eyes.

The girl would hesitate on that. "I can't tell you." She would know he wouldn't like that, and she would add, "But I've got plenty of money."

I wondered if Tony paid Larry a commission—so much for every "customer" he referred. No doubt Tony had a lot of contempt for Larry Preston, but it was a matter of professional courtesy.

Presently the meal was finished, and everyone stacked his or her dishes in the sink and started out the back door. Larry turned to me.

"Want to help me do up the pipe?"

"Sure." Now we would be alone for a moment.

I expected Larry to have some complex and expensive pipe, but he returned from the closet with nothing more exotic than a couple of empty gallon bottles, their corks drilled to accept two lengths of copper tubing. They made simple but effective water pipes.

We went to the sink to fill them.

I decided to open on a bantering note. "You seem to be doing pretty well in your chosen trade, man."

He grinned. "Better living through chemistry, man. That's always been my motto."

He had a way with clichés.

"What sort of stuff do you deal?"

"Grass, hash, mostly. I was really into hallucinogens for a while, but it got to be a hassle, and like, you know, the market's really changing."

The last part sounded familiar, and then I remembered: Tony talked this way.

"Now people aren't into, you know, tripping like they used to be. They just like to mellow out on a little fine hash." He laughed. "And I can see where they're at. I couldn't agree more."

"You deal mostly to college kids?"

"Oh, mostly."

My heart was beginning to thump. I must not change the tempo or alter my tone as I asked the next question. I looked down at the cork as Larry stuck it in the bottle and said, "You ever get into harder shit?"

He did not look up, and for a moment he did not answer. He was carefully arranging the tubing.

At last he said, "No, man. That screws people up. It's dangerous—it's a bad scene generally."

"But surely you've got contacts—you know people who deal heroin—" I stopped short. I expected Larry to turn and give me a long, careful look and ask, "Just what the hell are you getting at?"

But he only shook his head without looking up from the pipe. "Nope. Don't know anyone like that. You don't know much about the scene I'm into, Artie. Heroin's a big-time racket—those guys play rough. I don't know anything about that shit, and I want to keep it that way. Take the other pipe, will ya?"

And he turned and went out the door.

In the backyard everyone was sitting down in the traditional circle. The sun had long ago disappeared behind the tall trees to the west, leaving us in dim, grey dusk. There was a smell of earth in the air.

I sat down cross-legged and watched Larry cut up

a brick of hash. He had shown no hesitancy, no anxiety, no vehemence in his denials. Miserably I accepted it: I believed he had nothing to do with the old man. Time was running out, and I was getting nowhere.

It seemed incredible to me that I could know the old man was buying drugs—actually *have* the drugs, and still be incapable of causing him any trouble. It might just as well not have happened. I might just as well be sitting paralyzed with depression in a chair in his apartment, watching the sun go down and knowing I was through. And I had the same choices: I could let Tony's men find me and give them the boxes, then head west; or I could get the gun and end it. Either way, I had failed here, and I knew I must start back to the city.

I didn't. Instead, I sat there and got totally wrecked.

The girl beside me leaned forward to the bottle and drew. I listened to the smoke bubble up through the water for a moment, and then she swayed back, holding her breath, and vaguely edged the bottle my way.

I bent over and took a long hit, and passed it on.

It wasn't doing me any good. A lethargy had settled on my limbs and coated my brain, but the sharp edge of failure and depression would not be dulled.

I made a great effort and raised my head for the first time in half an hour.

It was now completely dark, a beautiful night. The stars glittered overhead, and a light wind rustled the new spring leaves around us. Two of the girls lay on their backs, as stoned as they wished to be. There were three of us still bending over this bottle—Larry, who was still, somehow, lucid enough to work with the knife and matches to keep the pipe going, the girl, and I.

The people on the other bottle were talking and laughing. Presently one of them got up and went into the house. In a moment the sound of George Harrison strumming his way through "My Sweet Lord" drifted out to us. Everybody laughed and applauded this feat.

I began to feel restless and rose, swaying; and lurched into the house. I have two choices, I thought. But I couldn't remember what they were. That was an improvement, anyway.

I went into the kitchen and poured some water down my parched throat.

"The smoke's pretty harsh, even with the water pipe, isn't it?" asked a girl's voice.

"Yeah," I said and didn't hear the word. Then I perceived that the stereo was on and quite loud in here. "Yeah!" I shouted.

The girl was standing at the cupboard, putting away dishes. When a crowd of people is smoking dope, there is usually some responsible soul who stays fairly straight, and here she was the one. She turned to me and smiled. She was not very pretty, but she had a good smile. A perfect, even row of white teeth and large green eyes that crinkled at the corners. She looked familiar to me.

"You don't remember me, do you, Arthur?" she asked on cue.

"No," I said. I was too far gone to be polite.

"I was at Chaffee when you were at Loomis."

I took that in, and presently it occurred to me to ask, "What year?"

"Same as you—'67." She stepped closer to me so that we would not have to shout. "You were pretty well known senior year, you know, because of those articles in the *Log*. You were really ahead of us on the war and all."

I vaguely remembered some fatuous and angry editorials, long debates with our faculty advisor.

"That was a long time ago."

"You went to Columbia, didn't you?" she went on. I was beginning to feel embarrassed that I knew nothing about her.

"Yes."

"Were you involved in the '68 thing?"

I nodded. "I was expelled because of it."

Her eyes widened. "Oh, wow. Like I didn't know they expelled people for that."

I didn't want to go into it. "What's your name?"

"Liz," she answered and looked away ruefully. "I went to U. Conn for a while, and then I just dropped out. I wasn't into anything political."

"Never mind. That's all over now."

"Oh, no, it isn't," she said earnestly. "There's going to be a big march on Washington soon to protest the Laos invasion. I'm going to be there."

"Good for you," I said and collapsed into a chair. Something nagged at me and made me ask, "Do you know Larry well?"

"No," she said. "I'm just crashing here 'cause my 'rents threw me out."

I nodded. I was really too numb to care about Larry any more.

"What's going on outside?"

I let her pull me to my feet. I was beginning to feel worse and worse, and wanted to keep moving.

"I don't know. Let's go out and see."

We stepped out on the porch and could see no one on the dark lawn. Liz went back in, turned off the record player, and returned.

"Larry?" she called.

"Down here," a voice called from the darkness, "at the pond." As we rounded a clump of rushes, I saw pale figures stepping out of dark clothes.

"Wonderful," I said. "A little skinny-dipping."

Liz laughed. "Larry was at Woodstock, you know, and since then he's been really into skinny-dipping. He says it's peaceful and beautiful, and you meet the right kind of chicks that way."

We both laughed. She was pulling the shirt over her head; she was the right kind of chick.

Maybe she would be the right kind for me. I had to do something as the dope wore off, and I was miserable. Maybe it would help me to get laid, or at least it would put something off.

I stripped quickly and looked at Liz. She was standing in the shadow of a tree, half turned away, pulling off her pants. Then she tossed them aside and stepped into the moonlight. I could see her small breasts and the dark hair between her legs.

There were chirps of alarm and little splashes as the frogs dove into the water at our approach. The evening wind, which only a week before would have borne a stinging chill, tonight felt soft and warm as breath on my bare back.

There was a splash as one white form disappeared into the dark water, then a shriek.

Larry laughed. "Cold, huh?"

"Sure is!" said the girl's voice breathlessly.

I reached the water's edge and ran quickly in, diving forward, and my heart jolted as the bitterly cold water cut into me.

I stood and turned to Liz. "Enough of that," I said and started back to shore. She grinned, being very careful to look up into my face, as skinny-dipping etiquette required.

I walked quickly back to where we had left our clothes. I was shivering violently and, worse, beginning to get straight. I had to push memories away, dully and continually, like a man slapping at mosquitoes in his sleep.

Already another white form had joined me, and I recognized Beth. I shrugged off my gathering thoughts and looked at her.

She was rubbing her breasts and shoulders with her shirt.

"Trying to get the old circulation going," she told me.

I nodded and started to pull on my pants. But Beth, when she had finished drying herself, dropped the shirt and sat down. I felt a stirring in the loins and was glad I had my pants on. Desire spread warmly through me, and I determined to think of nothing but bedding Liz for the rest of the evening. With her beside me, I might even be able to sleep and put the other things off until morning. Dimly I hoped that things would look better then, and dimly I knew that they wouldn't.

Presently the others came running up to dry off and joke at Beth and me for our lack of hardiness. I glanced at Liz as she stepped into her jeans. She had full, smooth hips, and just enough of her tan remained to show the white band across her buttocks where her bathing suit had been.

"Say," Larry called out, "like who's got the munchies?"

Everyone laughed and began to talk lovingly of pizza. After a long, rather incoherent discussion, it was decided to send Liz and me into town—Liz because she was straight and me because my car was the first out. I liked the arrangement.

Liz got up and gave me her pleasant smile. "I'll call the pizza place and order. Meet you at the car." I nodded, and she started off toward the house, carelessly stuffing her panties in her back pocket.

I concentrated hard and drove quite well back onto the state road and along it to the shopping center. I turned in, and Liz directed me across a vast, dark parking lot to the bright windows of the pizza joint.

"Just pull up in front," said Liz. "I'll go get them." As she left the car, I thought how kind and efficient she was. In a moment she came out with the two thin cardboard boxes, and we started back.

We drove along in silence for a while. I was trying to organize my thoughts enough to begin an easy, intimate conversation on which we could drift into bed. But Liz spoke first.

"What did they expel you for? Columbia, I mean."

"Sitting in at the president's office."

"But there were a lot of kids there. They didn't all get expelled, did they?"

I sighed. Liz knew a little about the strike, apparently, and I was too tired to think of a story, so I told her the truth.

"Columbia didn't expel me. My father did."

She turned to me, and her face in the dim light showed shock and concern.

"Oh, my God! How did it happen?"

I hesitated to tell her the whole story; it was bound to depress me. But, I decided, it would also make her feel sorry for me and more willing to go to bed with me.

"When they—the pigs—cleared the building I got arrested, and my father somehow found out about it —he's got contacts everywhere. So he ordered me home as soon as I was released.

"I went to his office in Hartford, and he, well, he surprised me. He didn't look angry or start to lecture me. He just asked me to sit down and explain why I was trying to shut down Columbia. So I started to tell him about its racist labor practices and all the slums it owned and how it was involved in the war. He listened and nodded and finally just said, 'But isn't Columbia more important to you in its role as an educational institution right now?' I told him no, it wasn't. It was more important to strike against it because of the racist, imperialist machine it represented."

"Right on!" said Liz. "Good for you!"

"Oh, I really let him have it. Then he just nodded and said mildly, 'In that case, I can't see why you should be a student at all, do you?' And he smiled. He had me, you know. He just gave me plenty of rope, and I did the job for him. He told me he wouldn't give me any more tuition money, and I was on my own."

Liz sat in stunned silence for a moment, and then she breathed, "Holy shit!" She turned to me urgently. "But everybody's parents *threaten* to do that—he wouldn't go through with it—I mean, there's the draft—"

"Sure he went through with it. He's no sentimentalist."

"But your mother—"

"My mother's dead."

"Oh," said Liz, and we were silent as the car crunched up the gravel road to the house. I tried to push away the memory of that interview with the old man, but with each moment it became more vivid. Again and again I saw him smile that cold, ironic smile he wore when he had won a point. I stopped the car and jumped out of it, trying to escape.

There were no lights on in the house, and I followed Liz around to the backyard. No one there. I supposed the party had raided the refrigerator, then paired off and gone to bed. Good. I wanted this girl now; I wanted to empty my mind and attend only to my senses. I turned to her.

She was looking ruefully at the grease-stained boxes in her hands. "I guess they're all ours," she said.

We went back to the house. Somewhere a girl was moaning softly, rhythmically. We exchanged a glance. Liz turned to open a door and looked in cautiously.

"There's no one in here," she said and turned on a light.

We went in, and she sat down on the floor and opened the first carton. The pizza looked good, and I realized I was very hungry. We went through it in total silence.

When the last piece was divided and eaten, Liz leaned back against the bed and patted her belly.

"I don't know about drugs heightening your level of consciousness, but dope really heightens my appreciation of pizza."

I laughed. I really liked her, and I looked at her thrown-back head, the line of her throat, her crossed legs. I knew I should never have told the story of my expulsion; swiftly and relentlessly, my mind was lining up the memories: the wanderings around the country, the return, the gun. I remembered that I had no excuse to be alive now.

I looked at her hips and forced myself to think of her body, bare beneath the soft denim. She raised her head and looked at me, and I slid over beside her and put my arms around her.

I knew at once that it was no good. She let me kiss her and caress her body; she even put her hands on my shoulders. But her embrace was without tension, without want. After a while she leaned back, away from me, took my hand from her breast. She held it, though. She was very kind, really.

"Arthur, I—you know—"

"That's all right. I don't feel like it either." I leaned back against the bed beside her.

"I'm sorry. You've looked like you were really down all night. You weren't getting stoned at all . . . not like it was doing you any good."

"I'm used to it," I replied. "I've been pretty down all my life. Except for a couple of months." There is nothing like a mixture of dope and despair for bringing down your reserve.

She leaned closer to me, speaking gently. Girls are always so solicitous after they refuse to sleep with me.

"When was that—when you were happy?"

"Summer of senior year," I said simply. I didn't feel like talking about it.

"Oh," she said at once. "You were with Claire Cowan then."

I started and looked at her. I had forgotten she was in Claire's class at Chaffee.

"Yeah."

"She was mostly real quiet, but you could tell she

had her head on straight. She was really smart, really beautiful."

"Yeah." In a moment she would ask me what Claire was doing now, and I did not want to answer that. I turned to her and said briskly, "You take the bed; I'll take the floor."

"Oh, no. I don't mind the floor at all, and you look really tired."

"Thanks," I said and crawled onto the bed. I *was* really tired; depression had sapped my strength; I was running down. Maybe I would be able to sleep after all.

Liz turned off the light.

"Good-night, Arthur."

"Good-night."

I knew that I would have to go to sleep at once, and I started to try to yield to fatigue.

It did not work, of course. I lay in the dark and presently I began to think about Claire. But not about the way she was now. I remembered how we had met.

That spring was very hard for me. I could forget about my mother during the day at school—I had a lot of work and a lot of interests. But at night I would go back to that huge, silent, empty house. My father stayed at the office even later than usual. I would settle down to homework, and then I would start to think about her at the hospital. It seemed wrong that I should be in the house, her house, when she couldn't be.

So most evenings I ended up driving out to Wentworth Mem. When she wasn't up to seeing me, I just sat down at a table in the cafeteria with my books. I could fail math anywhere, and I thought I might as well stay.

I was totally unaware of what an ostentatiously wretched figure I presented. People would see me alone at my table every evening and ask their doctors about me and think that it was very sad. I never looked up from my trig, never saw their sympathetic faces.

One night, when X and Y had eluded me once more, I did look up and saw a girl with long dark-gold hair and a grave, beautiful face waiting shyly before the table.

She swallowed nervously, put a smile on. "Arthur?"

"Yes."

"I'm Claire Cowan, Dr. Cowan's daughter." She gestured vaguely with her teacup. "He—you know—he pointed you out to me." Her smile slipped, and she looked down; she couldn't think of anything more to say.

I had a moment of insight—she must have seen me here often and thought that someone should talk to me. Finally she had taken it upon herself, and now she felt awkward and embarrassed. I would have liked to help her, but I just wasn't up to it.

We looked at each other a moment, and she said, "You go to Loomis, don't you?"

"Yes."

"I go to Chaffee."

I nodded, and again there was nothing to say. I thought that now she would surely turn away, and I realized that I wanted very much to talk to her. I clawed at my memory, trying to bring out some trifling comment or question, but nothing came. Then I heard her voice again.

"I know this is all really hard for you."

And that was all it took. I was never a stoical character; I was used to pouring out all my troubles to my mother. Now, I told Claire everything, talking for a long time about the ravages of the disease, and the cruel, frustrating treatments, and the endless waiting. She nodded, supplied the endings of my sentences when I stumbled, and always watched me with her gentle, deep-blue eyes.

At last I paused and realized that she had been

standing all this time. I asked her to sit down, and we talked about other things for a while. I noticed that she had a curious habit: she left the plastic lid on her teacup and sloshed the tea out of the air holes a sip at a time. Later I learned that she had started doing this to keep her tea warm during long nights of studying, when she was all alone and didn't care how it looked. I grew to love it, as I loved everything about Claire.

She was different then. People at Loomis knew her only vaguely as a good-looking grind who always refused dates because she had to study. "I have not been a great success as a teenager," she said to me once.

It was a characteristic remark. Claire's very frankness seemed intended to keep others at a distance. "I know what my problems are," she seemed to be saying, "and I can deal with them."

I found her self-sufficiency impressive and a little baffling; I knew what my problems were, too, but I doubted very much whether I could deal with them. So, for a while, our talks were like that first meeting, concerned entirely with my difficulties.

It was only when I began taking Claire home regularly that I came to understand her. Tom Cowan, if he was in one of his amiable moods, would go to get us all a beer. That meant running his wife's sniper fire in the kitchen. Claire and I would sit in the living room and hear her harsh, drawling voice. She talked to him as if he were an alcoholic even though he seldom drank more than two beers. But then, those beers were enough to completely erode what little attention he could give to matters outside the hospital: if he was drinking, he quickly came to ignore her barbs.

So she would make the most of what time she had, and Claire and I would sit together on the sofa, talk loudly, and pretend not to hear her.

But then one night, Claire dropped the pretense. She leaned close to me and spoke softly, sadly.

"It's been like this for so long." She stopped a moment, thinking. "She wants to make him feel guilty, and he does—and—and that's all. They'll never get any better—they just won't *try* to make their lives better."

I felt a tightness in my throat and put my arms around her. I understood; I knew what a burden she had carried. We were both only children; we had grown up in the solitary company of our own thoughts, in the big, empty houses our parents had once thought would make them happy.

And then, for a whole summer, we had each other.

I remembered last night, how I had gotten Tom to talk about his wife in order to embarrass Claire.

I hadn't cried myself to sleep since I was ten. It still worked pretty well.

9

For a moment I did not know what had awakened me.

A light rain was falling on the leaves outside the window, and enough light seeped under the shades so that I could see Liz, curled up on the floor, snoring lightly and peacefully.

But there was another sound.

I got up and crossed the room quietly. There were voices in the house, soft voices but with an edge of tension. I opened the door a little, listening.

Larry was speaking. "O.K. Like, you know, I like understand. But, you know, like there's nothing I can do. O.K.?"

Larry said "O.K." and "you know" a lot. The more upset and inarticulate he became, the more he said them. And right now, he was very uspet. I edged out into the hall, listening for the other voice.

"But you've got to help me—please—one shot—"

It was my father's girlfriend.

"Look, I haven't got any of that shit—like none at all. O.K.?"

Silence for a moment.

"I know what happens in withdrawal—"

"Like keep your voice down. O.K.?"

"First your eyes start tearing. You can't sleep. In about five or six hours you get gooseflesh, tremors in the limbs." She had not lowered her voice. She spoke in hard, flat tones, emotionlessly, like a doctor reciting symptoms. "After eight hours it starts to get really bad. Nausea sets in. Cramps. You get fever and chills. You vomit. Eventually you go into spasms. You're helpless—"

Larry cut in softly and urgently, telling her again that he didn't have any heroin. He was still speaking when I stepped around the corner.

They were standing at the open front door. The girl had her back to me. Her hair hung in dark, wet tangles on her white raincoat. Larry's mouth was working. His eyes widened when he saw me, and the girl turned. It hurt me to see the fear in that lovely face with its clear, blue eyes. Fear of me.

They just stood there in shocked silence for a moment, and then the girl turned and ran out the door. I heard a car starting up outside.

I was relieved that she was gone. I had feared briefly that she would ask me for the boxes, and I didn't think I could refuse her again. But now I was free to concentrate on Larry.

He shrank away from me as I approached him. With good reason, if I looked as angry as I felt. I pushed him out the screen door and slammed him against the post of the front porch.

"So you don't deal hard stuff?"

"I don't, man. I really don't. I wasn't bullshitting that girl. I really don't have any!"

"But you know people who do. You know Tony. Are you partners or what?"

Larry shut his small brown eyes and shook his head vehemently. "No, man. I hate that guy!"

I let go of him and stepped back. "Tell me about it."

"The girl came to me a couple of months ago. She told me she needed hard stuff and—"

"How did she get your name?"

"I asked her, but she wouldn't say."

Of course not.

"I told her I couldn't help her, but she was really desperate. She said she had to get some—"

"And she had plenty of money."

He shook his head some more. "No, man, really. I didn't take any bread from her at all."

"Sure. Tony paid you off, didn't he? When you delivered a new client to him."

Larry spread his hands in appeal. "Look, man. I'm not partners with this guy Tony. I just know his name. He's like mostly into pills, but—"

"But you heard he can supply a little shit on the side?"

"Yeah, right. I just told her how to reach him. That's all there is to it. Like I never saw her again after that one time. O.K.?"

"O.K." I turned to go back in.

"Hey, Artie," he called, "you like know this girl? Is she a friend of yours?"

"Yes," I said without knowing why.

"Hey, I'm like really sorry to hear that. She's really screwed up, but like it's not my fault. . . ."

I went back into the bedroom and got my coat. Liz turned over and looked sleepily up at me.

"See you, Arthur," she said vaguely, then added, "Good luck."

"Thanks," I said and went out. Larry watched me go past in silence, a darker flush than usual on his smooth, boyish cheeks.

I drove down the Taconic Parkway, through the grey rain, and I felt fine. I knew what to do.

Larry, of course, was of no use to me. He could not prove that the old man was buying drugs. The bastard had shrewdly kept himself out of it. He had sent the girl to see the pushers and Claire to make the pickup.

So only Claire could help me.

I knew she would. I had been so hurt and embittered to find her working for Maitland, Ruthven, Lavien, and Stewart that I had thought she had sold out utterly. Now it astonished me that I could assume that Claire, Claire whom I had loved, was capable of running heroin for the old man. Of course, she had no idea what was in the packages he had asked her to pick up.

I was going to see her now. First I would apologize for that shameful performance on the Cowans' front porch. At the time I had not been interested in the truth. I had wanted only to torment her, frighten her with unspoken suspicions. Now I would be completely open, show her that I still trusted her.

And I did. Of course, we could never get back together—it was pathetic even to think of that now—but I wanted to end the bitterness between us.

When she found out how he had used her, she would be as angry at the old bastard as I was. And together we would get him.

I heard a thud as I opened the door of the apartment; it had knocked something over. I looked in and saw a suitcase lying on the floor. My father had returned.

I fought an urge to duck out and go straight to Maitland, Ruthven, looking for Claire. But instead I closed the door behind me. I would not run. Today he had a lot more to fear from me than I from him. My heart thumping, I crossed the hall and the living room, and peered anxiously into the kitchen, the bedroom, and the bath.

The apartment was empty. He must have gone directly to his office.

I shrugged. It was just as well to postpone our confrontation until I had him cold. I picked up the phone and dialed.

"Good morning. Maitland, Ruthven." I recognized Randi's voice.

"Is Claire Cowan in the office?"

"I'm sorry, Claire's gone home for lunch today."

Good. It would be easier to talk to her away from the office.

"What's her home address, please?"

Randi hesitated. This must be against regulations.

"For what reason do you want to speak to her, sir?"

I was about to say, "Come on, Randi, you know me," and then I thought better of it. Right now the old man doesn't know where I am. Why tip him off?

"I'm a friend from Hartford. I just happened to be in town today and—"

That was reassuringly banal, and she gave me an address on West Seventy-second Street.

I went up the stairs of the subway station and walked the few steps to the corner of Seventy-second Street. The broad sidewalk sparkled like sandstone under the raindrops, and the horns and the pulsing rush of traffic were muffled in the soft heavy air. Across the street the trees in the park looked fresh and green. A young woman with a white umbrella stood on the corner, waiting for the light to change. As I passed I saw that her head was down and she was smiling to herself. I was glad that she had pleasant thoughts, and I felt cheerful.

I turned the corner and saw the green canopy with Claire's number on it. And just then she stepped out of the revolving door. She wore a tan raincoat and a broad-brimmed hat that framed her face. She, too, was smiling, and she looked beautiful.

The door revolved another quarter turn, and Jim Siegel stepped out.

I stopped dead, only a few feet away, and he was the first to see me. For a moment he looked startled, then he grinned, his teeth showing white against his dark, full beard. I had never been able to grow a beard.

"Mr. Lavien! Greetings, sir!"

Claire stood looking at us apprehensively as he came forward and extended a huge hand to me.

It always surprised me to find, when Jim stepped up to me, that we were eye to eye. He was just my height, six feet, but he seemed bigger—he was massively built. His great head, with its thick, curly hair and generous features, was borne on shoulders that looked a foot broad on either side and a chest that threatened to burst the top buttons of his shirt at his next breath. Perhaps that was why he left his shirts open, revealing a carpet of short, curling hairs over his collarbone.

I could feel my neck shrinking into my collar as he approached me. My neck is long and thin—I'm built like Audrey Hepburn—and I always feared that Jim would take his thick-fingered, thick-veined hand and snap it like a sparrow's. An absurd thought, as Jim was a gentle soul and would never harm a sparrow. Or me.

The illusion vanished completely as he took my hand in his weak grip. I noticed the palm was warm and moist; he was sweating.

"Well, Mr. Lavien, what brings you here today?" he asked in his deep, pleasant voice. There was anxiety in the lazy, heavy-lidded eyes behind his glasses, and I realized that beneath his habitual affability he was nervous facing me. This was, after all, the first time we had met since he had moved in on my girlfriend.

I remembered what I was here for and looked over the broad slope of his shoulder at Claire.

"I want to talk to you, Claire. It's rather important."

She raised her eyebrows in a good counterfeit of mild surprise.

"Sure. But we haven't got much time, and we have to go to the market for a few things." She glanced at her watch—no doubt she had to be back at Maitland, Ruthven soon—and took a tentative step toward Broadway. Then she caught the look in my eyes and said quickly, "We can talk when we get back. I'm sorry, but now that we're down here—"

I shrugged and fell into step beside them. Wimpy Jim grinned.

"You have to understand, Mr. Lavien, that getting down to the street from Claire's apartment is a major undertaking, requiring patience, courage—"

"Oh, indeed? Courage, you say?" Claire looked at him sideways, teasing him.

"To face the young ladies in white leather boots and the swarthy guys with bulges under their arms and other typical West Side transients who frequent your elevators."

Dimples sank into Claire's cheeks as her grin widened. "My building has its unsavory elements, to be sure, but no building in New York—"

"No building in *this* neighborhood—"

"I am only half a block away from one of the most chic areas in the city." She turned and gestured behind us at the Dakota, a massive French chateau, misplaced in time and space, that stood on the corner, looking elegant and unabashed under a coat of black soot.

Jim turned away from it, with a knowing smirk. "You can't fool me about that building. That's where the Devil lives when he's in town. I saw *Rosemary's Baby*."

Here the debate became theological. They walked along arm in arm, their heads bent against the rain, joking with the ease of familiarity.

I knew the routine, of course. I used to banter with Claire just like this in the old days. But today something was wrong. They seemed to force the pace, to be overelaborate, as if they wished to fill the time on the way to the store to prevent my saying anything. And Claire *should* be a little worried. She had called ALsr two days ago, turned the matter over to him, and here I was again, as ready to talk as I had been on her father's front porch. No doubt she was already thinking of calling the old bastard again. She would feel differently once I told her what those boxes contained.

* * *

We went into a Gristede's on Broadway. The over-heating practically raised steam off our soggy rain-coats. The shelves were brilliant with the works of America's packaging experts competing for our attention, all against a background din of cash registers and cans falling into carts. I felt a sense of unreality. It was so incongruous to stand beside this young woman, seemingly concerned only with Dijon mustard and macadamia nuts, and realize that unless I could get through to her, I might be dead in a few hours. I had not forgotten: today was the deadline Tony had set me.

Jim got a cart and wheeled it over to the side of the aisle, taking the items that Claire had collected out of her hands.

"Now, condiments. Would you advise yellow relish or green relish, Mr. Lavien? An important considera-tion when you have hot dogs every other night." He grabbed a jar of each.

Claire firmly took over the cart, put the relish back on the shelf, and, wrangling amiably with Jim, set off down the aisle.

My sense of incongruity had begun to turn to anger. Here was Claire, buying groceries and joking, when she had put my life in danger. For she had sent Tony to find me. Indirectly, unknowingly, but she had sent him just the same.

And yet she seemed completely unaware of me as she made her way through the dried beans and rice, comparing the cost of various brands of pasta. Wimpy at least knew I was here. He kept asking my opinion, drolly, of everything they bought.

I began to lose heart and hung back out of range of his cheerfulness as they went on to the freezers to get milk and sour cream.

I watched Claire pick up a carton. She asked Jim a question about it, and he came up to her. As they talked he absent-mindedly put his arm around her, and she, just as carelessly, covered his hand with her own. They began to examine the cheeses.

I would hold onto a scene like that through long, empty months, relive it until I had worn the memory threadbare. And they weren't even conscious of the moment as it passed.

Of course, they belonged to each other physically, as she and I never had. Jane Austen could have described our romance without a blush. Claire had been very discreet about her body. She had worn jeans and thick sweaters all through that spring, and I had felt a sort of warm surprise the first time I saw her in a bathing suit. I remembered still the shadowed hollow between her breasts as she bent over and the light dusting of freckles across her shoulders.

Only a few hours ago, she and Jim had been in bed together.

I turned away miserably and thought, Why should I be indignant? The brand of yogurt they buy is more important than whether I get killed or not, really. If Jim isn't satisfied, she'll want to get something he does like. If I die, who will care? They were a couple, their lives involved in every mundane decision of the day, each other. Everything one did mattered to the other. Nothing I did mattered to anyone.

I started to walk out of the store, out of their lives, and I took five agonized steps before the dear thought returned and wrapped itself around me like a warm blanket: you matter to someone; you matter to the old bastard. Or you will, because you're going to destroy him.

Claire and Wimpy were standing at the checkout counter.

"Mr. Lavien," Wimpy called, "can we draft you to carry a bag back to the apartment?"

"Sure," I said.

* * *

On the way up in the elevator, Claire and Wimpy had a long discussion about his laundry. He had brought down a bag of dirty clothes, forgotten about them, and now he had to return to Hartford and go back on duty at the hospital right away.

"You should have told me. We could have done it last night."

"Oh, never mind," said Jim affably. "The patients like interns to look a little disheveled—makes them think we're working hard."

I wondered if Claire would remember, years from now, that she had been worried about laundry a few moments before I told her the truth about Arthur Lavien, Sr.

We walked down a green hallway, papered in a dreary floral pattern, to Claire's door and stepped into the living room of her apartment. It was a pleasant place, with a view over the intricate gables and dormers of the Dakota's roof. There was a worn green sofa and a couple of deck chairs and a print of Van Gogh's sunflowers on the wall.

"Come on in the kitchen, Arthur, and we'll talk while we unpack."

"No, Claire," I said. "We're gonna put the damned bags down, and we're gonna talk now."

We looked at each other for a long moment. Then she gave an exasperated sigh and held her bag out to Jim.

"All right. Put this one away, will you, Jim? It's got the ice cream in it."

But Jim was watching me. He did not even notice the bag.

"I'd really prefer to stay, if Mr. Lavien doesn't mind."

At least he was getting the idea.

Claire put the bag down on the floor, folded her arms, and looked at me.

"Go ahead, Arthur."

I stepped closer, my eyes on her face.

"It's about those two packages—the ones I took from your car Wednesday night."

She was prepared for this and put on a look of total bewilderment.

"I don't know what you're talking about."

"Yeah, right. Your car was parked here all Wednesday night. We've been through this before, and it's time you dropped it. It just won't do any more."

She was cool, though. She shut her eyes and took a breath, trying to control her impatience.

"Look, I don't know what you're trying to—"

"Just be quiet, will you? When you've heard me out, you'll want to tell me the truth." I hurried on before she could interrupt. "As a matter of fact, I ran into the delivery boy that night. When he saw me, he pulled a knife. But I grabbed the boxes and ran. And now I know who they came from, and who they're for."

Now traces of alarm began to show through her pose of innocent bewilderment. She had not known the messenger boys carried knives.

"What boxes, Arthur?" She was still clinging to the pose.

"You really don't know, do you? You ran your little errand for the old man, and you never wanted to know what was inside those boxes. Well, I'll tell you. A few thousand dollars' worth of downers and some bags of heroin."

At last I had gotten through. She stared at me wide-eyed, opened her mouth, but found nothing to say. I came a step nearer to her, trying to speak gently now.

"I understand that you had no idea what you were doing for him. But now you know, and you've got to help me. I've still got the stuff and—"

Suddenly her hands flew to cover her face, and she turned away. There was a long silence; for a moment I thought she would begin to cry. But her shoulders relaxed and the hands slipped down. She had decided.

She spoke slowly and deliberately without looking at me.

"I have no idea what you're talking about. My car was parked outside this building."

"Please, Claire," I said softly, desperately. "This is your last chance. You can't stick by him any more."

She spun around, her face working. For a moment she looked as if she was going to tell me the truth, but then she gave in.

"I don't know what you're talking about!" she burst out furiously and closed her eyes.

Jim stepped up beside her. His face was very pale, his voice measured.

"Look, Arthur. whatever you're trying to pull, it isn't very funny."

Claire backed a step away from me, against Jim, and he put his arm around her.

So that was it. She knew everything, and still she sided with him.

"All right, damn it!" I roared. "I'm fucking tired of you all. I've got the stuff safe in a locker at Grand Central, and I'm gonna get it now. I'm gonna take it to the old bastard's office and dump it all over his desk!"

I spun around and started for the door.

"I hope he's in conference with a lot of his important assholes so they'll all see it. I'm gonna get him, and I hope you all go down with him!"

I turned. They stood motionless, watching me in silence. I threw open the door and ran out.

10

I was glad to see the taxis waiting in a long yellow row along Forty-second Street. Once I had the boxes, I would want to get downtown quickly.

I hurried down the ramp to the main concourse, past people listing sharply under the weight of their suitcases, and dodged between irascible travelers crowding around the information kiosk and dark-suited businessmen at the Merrill, Lynch booth. I was hardly aware of the grimy, musty station. My thoughts were already at Maitland, Ruthven.

I would cross the lobby at a dead run and hurtle down the stairs. I wanted to alarm the receptionist yet give her no time to warn him. I would throw open his office door—I could see his secretary rising startled from her desk—and charge into that large, quiet inner office. I hoped the secretary would follow—I hoped his office would be filled with people as I upended the box on his wide desk and spilled shiny blue pills all over it.

I reached the locker, put my hand in my pocket for the key—and only then did I remember to look behind me.

He was a few yards away, dodging around a group of women with shopping bags, his eyes fixed on me—the stocky man I had lost in the Village.

He had returned to U.N. Plaza and waited patiently until I returned this morning. And he had been following me ever since.

Fool, I thought, jamming the key into my pocket. I turned quickly and half ran to my left. There were crowds of office workers coming down the escalators from the Pan Am Building, and I fought my way through them, heading across the concourse to the arcades of shops and cafés. If I could lose him in the rush, duck out to Lexington Avenue . . .

You always know, even in a crowd of people, if someone is staring at you. I felt it, and scanned a group of travelers at one of the gates in front of me. Sure enough, I found myself looking into a thin, sharp-nosed face. It was the kid from Claire's car, the one with the knife. He was pushing his way through the crowd with the overhand motions of a swimmer, and his eyes were fixed insolently on me.

I veered to the right, saw a newsstand in front of me, strode toward it, and elbowed my way between a couple of men thumbing through papers.

I stood staring at a girl in a bikini on the cover of a magazine and felt them closing in behind me from both sides.

The man in front of me paid, and the clerk turned a sallow, coarse-pored face to me.

"Is there something you wanted, sir?"

I stared at him helplessly. "No, I—"

His tone changed. "Then clear out of the way, please."

I didn't move. The clerk was looking at me, as was the man to my left. For the moment they might keep me safe.

"What?" I said, stalling.

"Look, you're in the way. There are people trying to—"

"I want a copy of the *Times.*"

He peeled a copy off a stack and thrust it at me. "Fifteen cents."

"No, I want yesterday's *Times.* Could you look—"

He squinted irritably at me. "Yesterday's? Nah, we don't have any left. Now please clear out."

I felt that Tony's men were right behind me now, and suddenly my nerve broke. Foolishly I bolted.

My arm was grabbed hard at once. The kid was right beside me. I could smell his sweat and the wet wool of his jacket.

"Give me the key, man. Right now," he said in his soft unemphatic voice.

I looked down—both his hands were gripping my arm—no knife. I glanced around and saw his pal moving up on the other side. In a moment they would have me between them. They would trip me and pretend to help me up, grabbing for the pocket where they had seen me put the key.

The stocky guy was only a step away.

I jerked my arm free and hurled myself away from them.

And then I saw two blue-coated cops only a dozen yards away and broke into a dead run, right at them. They turned, nodded to each other, and started to move toward me. I thought, They know I'm in trouble; they know I need help.

But that wasn't it at all.

I stopped before them gasping, and before I could speak they grabbed me and threw me against the ledge of the information booth.

"Now don't make trouble, buddy," said a harsh Bronx voice at my ear. "Just lean on your hands and spread your feet apart."

Stupid cops, I thought. They see someone running and automatically they nail him and frisk him. But that was all right with me. Even now Tony's friends would be melting back into the crowd. I was safe. When the cops were satisfied that I had no weapon, they would let me go and ask what this was all about. I started working on a story, one that would tell them as little as possible.

Hands ran swiftly and smoothly down my arms, under my coat, and up my sides to the armpits. My eyes fell on the face of the information clerk behind the glass. He was bald and heavy-jowled, and he stared back at me blankly, like a fish in a tank.

A hand patted my coat pocket, dug into it, and closed around the key.

"Hey, Joe. He's got a locker key, all right."

Oh, no, I thought. Oh God, no!

They spun me around to face them. One was short and fat, and his jaw was shiny with the bristle of a thick, dark beard. The other was taller, with sandy hair and sandy eyebrows that gave him a benign look. He had my wallet in his hands.

"Mr. Lavien, we are detaining you on suspicion of possession of narcotics. You have the right to remain silent; however, if you choose to speak . . ."

He went on about my rights, but I didn't listen. I felt numb, absurdly light-headed. Some part of my mind worked at figuring out how this had happened, but I didn't listen to that either. For a while I looked at the little brass key in the fat cop's hairy hand, and then my gaze wandered up over his shoulder. People were passing by, walking sideways so that they could stare at me. It seemed strange to me that none of them averted their eyes when I stared back. I studied their faces: a youngish man with a neatly trimmed beard and an ugly birthmark over his right eye; a middle-aged woman in pink, with glasses as thick as the bottom of a Coke bottle. I noticed that they moved on until they were well past me, then stopped and looked back. A loose half circle was beginning to form around the information kiosk at a distance of about twenty feet. A tall black man in a tight-fitting jeans jacket walked past without glancing at me, broke through the circle, and went on to catch his train.

I was falling into a trance, beginning to feel like a bystander myself. I tried to concentrate, realized that the cops were arguing. Suddenly the fat one, Joe, turned away from his partner impatiently and grabbed me by the shoulder.

"O.K., kid, take us to this locker."

"No, Joe," said the younger man mildly. "We got to get a warrant before we can open the locker."

"Look, this guy fits the description the caller gave, and he's got the key. What more do we need?"

The younger man pushed the bill of his cap back and went on quietly. "Come on. We call the courthouse, get a warrant sworn out. It'll only take half an hour—"

"Why the hell bother?"

"If we don't, we might get the whole goddamn case thrown out of court six months from now, and it'll be a waste of time. We got to make sure."

He spoke with weary, determined authority. Joe glared at him a moment, then gave it up with a shrug. He wrenched me around by my arms, and I felt the cold touch of metal on my wrists and heard a click as the cuffs locked. Then the cops arranged themselves on either side of me and guided me up the ramp and out of the station as people stared at us.

I had lost interest in them now, lost interest in everything. Vaguely I thought, They'll put me in a chair in the station, they'll leave me, and the shock will slowly wear off. Then they'll come and get me and bring me back here, open up the locker, and take the boxes out. By that time I won't be numb. I'll know what's happening, and I'll be frightened. I wished they had gotten it over with.

There was a black and green squad car parked on the wet, grey street outside, and they put me in the back. The young cop got in behind the wheel while his partner picked up the radio receiver.

"A-four fifty-five to Dispatch. We have the three-o-one suspect in custody and are proceeding to station."

The radio barked acknowledgment, and we pulled

out onto Forty-second Street. There was a wire screen in front of me. I looked at the doors: no handles on the inside. I thought, This is the first of a series of locked rooms I will be put in, one after another, for— for how long?

I knew I did not have a chance. Thousands of dollars' worth of pills and heroin, a ridiculous story, no witnesses, no proof. And I was such a model citizen, too: long hair, no job, no money—a drifter. I even had a record—breaking and entering, refusing to obey an order to disperse, from Columbia. No, the pigs would have no problem putting me away.

We stopped alongside a row of parked squad cars, and the cops got out and opened my door. I stumbled getting out; I had never realized you need your hands to leave a car. The younger man helped me up, and they hurried me into a door and down a long corridor painted a poisonous green.

We went into a room with fluorescent lights and big, dirty windows. Short-sleeved detectives sat at long rows of desks, guns at their belts jabbing into the rolls of fat around their waists.

"I'll call the courthouse, get procedures started on the warrant," the younger cop said. The fat one nodded to him and he turned away.

In one corner of the room was a barred enclosure, like a cage at the zoo. I was led to the door.

The cop turned to a balding detective at a nearby desk. "Hey, Bill, open this thing up, will ya?"

The detective got up, picked a key out of a drawer, and went to the door. I turned to the fat cop. I had recovered a little, and there was one thing I wanted to know.

"The tip—the call you got—was it anonymous?"

Without looking at me he smiled, as if he had been expecting me to ask this all along. "Won't do you any good, kid. That doesn't matter in a case like this."

The tip had been anonymous.

The detective slid the door open, and I stepped in without waiting to be pushed. There were two benches. Across from me a Puerto Rican kid sat bent over with his elbows on his knees. Over the clatter of the typewriters I could hear him talking mournfully to himself in Spanish. He didn't look up as I sat down. The fat cop went to a desk in front of me, pulled a long form thick with carbons out of a drawer, and fitted it into his typewriter. Occasionally he looked up at me through the bars. Otherwise I was alone with my thoughts.

The tip had been anonymous. It was all quick and clean—the direct approach, ALsr's trademark. The moment I had left Claire's apartment, she had called him, told him what I was doing.

"Mr. Lavien, he said there were drugs in those boxes!"

He would grunt noncommittally. "We can discuss all that later, Claire, when there's time."

I could see him cradle the receiver, look out the window at the neighboring Wall Street towers. Did he think, I have worked all my life to get where I am now, and it is worth sending my son to jail, if necessary, to save myself?

No, he did not weigh things like that; he was a pragmatist. The problem was simple and serious: I was on the way to his office to create a scene; I had to be stopped; there was little time. He considered, and the solution came to him. He lifted the receiver.

"Claire, this is very important. Can you remember what Arthur was wearing?"

He took the description and hung up with a few empty assurances. Then he dialed the police.

"In a few minutes a tall, thin young man with very long dark hair, wearing a blue jacket and tan corduroys, will enter Grand Central Station. He is going to pick up a cache of drugs from one of the luggage lockers."

And then he put down the phone.

I had made it so easy for them. I heard my voice yelling at Claire, "I've got the stuff safe in a locker at Grand Central. . . ."

Why had I told her that?

I knew, of course. You miserable fool, you wanted her to know it all, to share in your triumph. Even then, you still insisted on believing she was on your side.

When Claire found out—not from the old man, of course—what he had done to me, she would be horrified. All through the long months that my trial would inevitably take, she would be miserable.

I knew, though, that she would be silent.

She was trapped. She couldn't help me without revealing that she had gone to pick up the drugs. She had not known then what she was doing, but that would not fully excuse her. Her career was at stake. And her career, like my father's, was more important than I was.

There was a brief lull in the clatter of typewriters. For a moment I listened to the sound of the rain on the pavement outside. Then the racket began again, and I returned to my thoughts. I wondered how this had happened to us, to Claire and me.

One hot day in September, I had gone over to the Cowans' to help pack up the station wagon. When it was done, Claire and I drank some lemonade in the kitchen, and then she went out and got in the car to go to Cambridge. Our romance ended at that moment, but I did not know it.

For six more months I hung on, learning to get by on less and less, trying not to realize that we were drifting apart. I wrote her long, earnest letters. Her answers were short in length and long in coming. I awaited them anxiously, and when I got one, it only depressed me. She would dismiss my opinions with curt irony, if she remembered to mention them at all, and launch into a record of her successes and activities, as brisk and impersonal as a newsletter. Finally I would decide to call her, only to be told that she was "at the *Crimson*" or "at Government Center." When I put down the receiver, the black plastic would be shiny with sweat marks, and my hand would ache from the strain of my grip.

When I did reach her, it was even worse. Early in the spring I called to tell her about a peace march being held in New York and asked her to come down. "Oh, I really think I'm more valuable to society as a student than as a marcher at this point," she replied airily.

As the months passed, she became more and more taken up with her committees and cocktail parties, and had less and less time for an "impractical" radical like me. When it counted, she had no time at all.

I remembered that day in May, the day my father told me he could see no point in financing my education further, and disowned me. During the train ride down from Hartford I was too busy raging at him to worry; but when I got back to my apartment, I realized that I did not have enough money to pay next month's rent and that my draft deferment would run out in a few months. I paced frantically across my room for a long time, too angry and frightened to think what to do next. Finally I called Claire.

"Um—Claire's very busy right now," said her roommate doubtfully. "Who's calling?"

"Arthur Lavien."

"Oh. Just a minute."

I always got that reaction, and I was proud of it. People knew I was above the swirl of Claire's busy life; I got special treatment. Only later did I begin to think it was the same sort of special treatment my mother had gotten at Wentworth. Everyone felt sorry for a hopeless case.

Claire came on the line, sounding, as always, precise but rather distant.

"Claire, can you come down? I have to see you."

She couldn't.

"Well, then, can I come up there?"

Right now? Today?

"Yes, damn it, today!"

She sighed and explained patiently that it wouldn't be much fun for me; she was very busy. She told me about the various meetings she had scheduled, and there was a party that night—

"Look, I don't give a damn about your meetings and your party now! Can you stop ego-tripping long enough to talk to me?"

Silence. I hoped I had made her angry. I wanted some kind of response. But in a moment the low, even voice resumed. She had to go out right now, but if I could wait, she could call me in an hour and we could talk, all right?

I said that was fine and hung up. I felt so happy. Any crumb she gave me satisfied me, made me grateful.

I sat motionlessly by the phone for that entire hour. For the first twenty minutes I was eagerly thinking things out, making my problems clear to myself so that I could make them clear to her. I knew she would help me. We had a lot of trouble getting together, but once we *were* together, we always talked things out. I stared at the telephone, waiting for it to ring, to pick it up and hear her voice on the other end.

Presently I looked at my watch—half an hour had passed. Suddenly, terribly, I knew that the phone was not going to ring. She had forgotten to call me back. Forgotten, or did not care to make the effort.

But I sat by the phone for thirty more humiliating minutes. When the allotted hour was up, I stood. I was not going to call her again. I was not going to wait another minute. Claire Cowan had let me down on one occasion too many now, and I was through with her.

I hurriedly packed a knapsack and a sleeping bag, left a note on the stereo asking my roommates to return it to the old man, and walked out of the apartment.

I felt fine as I started west. The fascist creeps who ran Columbia, the pigs who had arrested me, the old bastard who had handed me over to the draft board, were all part of the same machine. Claire too was part of it. I knew it at last, and I was free. It was simple: all I had to do was run.

Three years later I came back for a gun.

Now I sat on the wooden bench and looked out through the bars at the fat cop typing my arrest record and felt saturated with failure. I had been given one last chance. All along I had known that my father's busy, successful life was rotten underneath, and I had held the proof in my hands. He had tried to frighten me into surrender, but I had beaten him with the weapon of my despair—won because I did not care what happened to me.

And then I had thrown it all away by yielding to one last empty hope. I had believed, again, that Claire was on my side. And, again, she had betrayed me.

It wasn't a matter of the good guys and bad guys, Establishment or Anti-Establishment: Claire and the old bastard were simply winners. And I had proven myself a loser for the last time.

PART TWO

11

The barred door slid open, and I looked up.

Would I have to go back to the station already?

It was a different cop, a middle-aged man with stripes on his sleeves. He had tired, watchful eyes and a luxuriant grey mustache. He held a yellow paper in his hand.

"Arthur Lavien, Junior?"

I stood. He looked at me, at the paper again, and then put it away.

"Turn around, please."

I turned and heard a click as the handcuffs were unlocked. The heavy metal rings slid away from my wrists.

"I'm instructed to take you down to the courthouse, Mr. Lavien. Come with me, please."

He led the way out of the squad room. The fat cop, the one named Joe, sat at his desk, putting papers away in a drawer. He did not look up as we passed.

Outside the rain had let up. I was put in the back of another squad car. The middle-aged sergeant got in front.

"Courthouse," he said to the driver. "Back entrance."

I knew this had something to do with the search warrant, but I did not know why I was needed, and I did not care. I just looked out at the leaden sky and listened to the cops talking about baseball and the radio giving out numbers, codes, and addresses.

Presently we turned onto Centre Street and drove

past the monumental stairway and colonnades of the courthouse. Then we turned again, into a garage entrance.

The sergeant got out and opened my door, and led me into an elevator with peeling green walls and cigarette butts crushed into the floor. He pressed Five.

The doors opened onto a long, quiet hallway. We walked along white wainscotted walls with tall windows overlooking the city hall park on one side and dark wood doors on the other.

The sergeant stopped and knocked on a door that read Hon. Samuel Richards. A woman's voice called, "Come in."

We stepped into a small anteroom. A secretary looked up.

"It's about the three-o-one this morning. Grand Central—" began the sergeant.

"Yes. This is Mr. Lavien?"

The sergeant nodded, and we were told to go in.

The Judge's office was small, paneled richly in wood grown satiny with age. There were heavy green draperies and two matching green leather chairs turned toward a broad desk. Behind the desk sat Judge Richards, a man in his late forties, with dark hair and dark-rimmed glasses. Curiously, he smiled at me as I came in.

Standing in front of the desk was a square-jawed, red-faced man. His hands were in his pockets, dragging back his coat to show a gun at his belt: a detective. He was not smiling.

"Thank you, Sergeant. You may wait outside," said the Judge in an authoritative voice. He looked at me again. "Sit down, Mr. Lavien."

There was somebody sitting in the right-hand chair, so I took the left, glancing at the man beside me. It was my father.

He had been so vividly present in my thoughts for the last two days that the sight of him, here, now, when I least expected it, literally stunned me. For a long time I stared at him and could neither move nor think.

My father always wore half-rimmed glasses; the frames hid his eyes when he looked at you.

"Ah, Arthur," he said, then cleared his throat, shrugged, and looked at the floor.

It was his habitual gesture on meeting me, and it snapped me out of my stupor. What is he doing *here?* I wondered. Come to play the concerned parent while making sure I was put away good and proper? But that made no sense. He would surely want to keep himself out of this; let the law take its course. . . .

My reasoning rambled hollowly on, and I ceased to pay it any attention. It was enough that the man had suddenly appeared and knocked the props from my theories. As the silence continued, I stared at his averted face with a kind of fascination.

I had forgotten in three years how alike we looked. Friends and relatives had always said so, and it was obvious to me as well, because the similarity was one of features, not of expression. Our faces were thin and angular, with a high cliff of forehead, an obstinate block of chin, and a long, ungainly nose. I hoped that was the end of it—certainly I smiled more often than he. But it had always bothered me that Arthur Lavien, Sr., had given me not only his name but also his looks.

Now I watched him and wondered what he had come here to do.

Judge Richards spoke. "You were saying, Mr. Lavien?"

"Yes." My father leaned forward but did not look up. "We are dealing with an anonymous tip here, as I understand it."

He sighed disdainfully and glanced at the yellow legal pad in his lap. "Allow me to quote from the ruling of the New York Court of Appeals, in the case *State v. Callahan,* 232 N.Y.S. 2d 532 (1969): 'If the police have no idea who their informant is, if they do not know how he received his information, or on what he based his "tip," they cannot know whether the informant is credible or the information reliable. Therefore they have no probable cause for arrest.'" He looked up at the detective. "You have no probable cause in this case, Lieutenant."

My God, I thought, he's trying to get me off.

Judge Richards nodded and turned to the detective. "As Mr. Lavien has said, this case involved the illegal searching of a car, but I think the ruling is equally relevant to a luggage locker."

The detective took his hands out of his pockets and tugged his coat over the gun. "This is all highly irregular, Judge Richards. I'm not prepared to argue a case—"

"You have no case," interrupted my father, slowly and contemptuously. "*If* you get a warrant, *if* you open this locker and find, let's say, a load of heroin"— his voice rose contemptuously on the word—"the case will be thrown out of court because you will not be able to show probable cause." He stood and buttoned his coat. "So why don't we save everyone a good deal of money and embarrassment, and drop the whole matter right now?"

He's going to pull it off, I thought. He's going to keep them away from that locker and see that I go free.

But why? Why was he trying to spring me if he had turned me in himself?

Because he had not turned me in, had not made that phone call. Swiftly, dizzily, the world I had been living in for the last two days turned upside down.

The lieutenant was speaking, angrily, loudly. "He behaved suspiciously. He was running—"

"*Toward* the police, as I understand it."

The lieutenant started to speak, broke off, looked from Judge Richards to my father and back again.

The Judge smiled. "I think, on the whole, it would be a good idea to forget this one, Lieutenant."

"You won't issue the search warrant?"

"I think not."

The lieutenant turned away, grabbing up his raincoat. Then he paused a moment, dug furiously in his pocket for something, and tossed it in my lap.

I picked it up as he went out: the key.

There was a moment's silence, and then my father and the Judge looked at each other and laughed.

"That is the most irregular judicial procedure at which I have ever presided," said Judge Richards. Then, still chuckling, he stood and reached a hand across the table to me. After a moment's confusion, I took it.

"Well, young man, you seem to have either a bitter enemy or a friend with a warped sense of humor."

"Oh," I replied, "the, uh, the informant." And I laughed, too.

With almost perceptible relief my father removed his smile. "Thank you very much, Sam. This silly episode might have turned out very badly."

"Not at all, Arthur. As you said, you've saved everyone a good deal of time and embarrassment."

They shook hands and agreed to meet in Mamaroneck for golf the following weekend. Then we were out the door.

In a daze I followed his broad pin-striped back down the hall. He stopped at the elevator and pressed the call button, and addressed me without turning.

"We're lucky it rained."

He always began that way, to force you to ask him questions. It gave him control of the conversation.

"Why?"

"Because if it had not, Sam would have been out playing golf this afternoon, and the whole matter would have been rather more difficult to arrange."

So this is the way he does it, I thought. If I were

some Puerto Rican kid, if I were anybody but his son, I still could have gotten off, but only after months of trial and appeal. ALsr had achieved the same result in five minutes.

"Is there really a load of heroin and pills in the locker?"

He still faced the elevator. I stepped around to look at his face. "You didn't know?"

He looked at me sideways and impatiently tugged off his glasses. His eyes were grey-green, habitually narrowed—again, like mine.

"No, Arthur, I didn't know anything about this until Claire Cowan called me an hour ago," he began, in a bored, exasperated voice. "She was very upset. She said you'd left her place after accusing her of running drugs, or picking up drugs, or something, for me, and that you were on your way to confront me. Well, I was looking forward to that confrontation." His lips curled ironically. Once more I was amazed at his coldness. He was not hurt that I had suspected him of buying drugs; he was merely contemptuous of my shoddy and fantastic reasoning.

"When you didn't appear, I reasoned that you had gotten into trouble and started calling some friends of mine. We're very lucky it rained, all right."

The elevator doors opened and we stepped in. I tried desperately to gather my thoughts.

"Look, Dad," I burst out. "I've seen this girl!"

He was scanning the floor buttons. "What girl?"

"*Your* girl!"

He gave me another short, angled look. Then he raised his eyebrows and sighed, and looked away.

"If there is such a person as "my girl," she is a thirty-five-year-old industrial designer who's in Atlanta this week. Is that whom you mean?"

My mind was reeling. Claire had been telling me the truth all along—my father knew nothing about the drugs, had no connection with the girl. As the whole structure of evidence that I had risked my life to build up came tumbling down, I grasped at the one thing I was sure of.

"But—but the drugs *are* there!"

He nodded. "Claire wants to talk to you."

"Where is she?"

"She's coming here. You're to wait for her in the garage." He glanced at his watch. "And I have to get back to my office."

I stared at him. "You don't want to know more about this?"

He did not look at me. "I've already asked Claire if there was anything I could do, and she said no. Since she seems to be more affected by this mess than either of us, I think we should respect her wishes."

My father always had a great deal of respect for Claire.

We rode in silence to the first floor, and the doors opened.

"If you need me, call," he said, and walked out.

I felt I should say something, and I called, "Thanks, Dad." But the elevator doors had already closed.

I got out at the garage level and leaned against the wall beside the elevator. I felt the cool granite against my back and heard the rush of cars and the hum of the big lights and thought about nothing.

After a while the elevator doors slid open again and the mustached sergeant who had brought me here stepped out. He nodded to me, looking oddly embarrassed, and we stood side by side in silence until a squad car pulled up and he got in.

As it drove away I thought, The police are leaving me alone. And relief and exultation welled up inside me. It was a physical sensation: the joints of my limbs relaxed, and my back and shoulders straightened as the accumulated weight of tension and despair was lifted. You're free, I said to myself.

And Claire is innocent. I remembered our talks, on Wednesday night and this afternoon, with astonishment and shame. I had read calculation into her bewildered silences, cold-blooded duplicity into her simple denials. Never had she had the slightest idea what I was talking about, even when I had raged and cursed at her two hours earlier. And yet she had had the presence of mind to call ALsr and begin the process of setting me free. But for her, I would be in jail right now.

I heard the iron rattle of the Volvo's engine bouncing off the walls, and in a moment it swung around beside me. Claire leaned over to unlock the passenger door and glanced up at me. Her blue eyes were expressionless below the dark brows. Then she straightened up and was hidden by the line of the roof.

I got in and turned to her, searching for words to tell her how sorry and grateful I was.

But she spoke first. "I know nothing about this but what you've told me." She slipped the gear lever into first and looked around for the exit ramp. "I took the train to Hartford Wednesday night and didn't see my car until I got back to Manhattan and found it parked where I'd left it, on Seventy-second Street."

She spoke in a preoccupied, unemphatic way, as if she were giving all her attention to her driving. It took me off balance, and I was silent.

"Do you believe me?" she asked.

"Oh, Claire, of course I do!"

Her brusqueness hurt me, and I looked at her reproachfully.

But we had reached the exit, and she was leaning away, scanning the street for an opening in the traffic.

"Then that simplifies things a little," she said tersely. She turned and looked past me into the street, and at last I could see her face. She was very pale, and her lips were drawn tight with strain.

I understood then. My father had said, "She's more

affected by this mess than either of us." At the time
I had been too dazed to understand him; I had begun
to think that all the events of the last two days were
an illusion of my own.

But it had all happened. Someone had used Claire's
car to pick up a shipment of drugs. She had just dis-
covered this and obviously was in no mood to respond
to my feelings of relief and humble gratitude. The
pressure was off me simply because it had shifted to
her.

I looked out the windshield as we maneuvered
through the narrow streets of Little Italy, and tried to
be calm and businesslike. "You apparently don't want
to bring the police, or even my father, into this?"

"Your father really has nothing to do with it. And—
and I don't want to go to the police yet."

The low, even voice had faltered.

"You know who *did* have your car Wednesday
night?"

She answered promptly, "It had to have been Jim."

Jim. I thought of that cheerful, bearlike figure, am-
bling around the block in the dark as I fought the
kid with the knife.

"You're sure?"

"He was at my apartment all evening. He knows
where I keep the keys."

"And when you got back from Hartford?"

"He was asleep." She corrected herself. "I *thought*
he was asleep. He would have had plenty of time to
get back from Greenwich, with hours to spare."

While I stood on the Cowans' front porch threatening an uncomprehending Claire, he had brought the
car back to Manhattan and crawled deceitfully into
bed. I felt like a fool.

For a while we were silent as I sorted through the
wreckage of my theories, trying to find the fragments
of truth.

"Did you and he talk that night?" I asked.

"Yes. Obviously he said nothing about taking the car."

"But did you mention talking to me—that I had told you I'd seen the car?"

She thought a moment. "Yes, I did say something about it."

I turned in my seat eagerly. "He made a phone call right away, didn't he?"

"Not right away. I was with him." She thought for another moment. "But then I went to take a bath, so he could have." She glanced at me now. "Why?"

"He was giving my name to the pusher, the man he got the drugs from."

"You've seen the—the pusher?"

"Yes." I remembered Tony, his flat, brown eyes, his matter-of-fact tone as he told me that next time he would have the gun. By now his friends had reported to him that they had seen me arrested. At least I was safe from Tony, for a while.

Jim had sent him to me. Jim had known all along that I had the packages. I thought of his nervousness when he had first seen me on Seventy-second Street. But after that I had hardly glanced at him, had concentrated only on Claire.

And then I thought of something else that I had blamed on her, something else that Jim had done to me.

"*He* turned me in! He tipped off the cops!"

I was staring at Claire again. She nodded. "Yes," she agreed. "It had to have been he."

I felt a wave of fury at this pleasant weak-willed son of a bitch who had been ready to send me to jail. Absurdly, I was angry at Claire, too.

"What happened after I left your place? Did you go to take another bath?"

I nearly choked on the words as I said them. I had been given a bad scare and I was angry, but it was stupid and shameful to fire sarcasms at Claire. I started to apologize, but she gave me no time, speaking quickly and tonelessly.

"He left soon after you did. He said he had to get back to Hartford. He must have called the police from a pay phone."

I was incredulous. I remembered Claire staring after me with frightened eyes as I went out. How could Jim casually announce that he had to get back to Hartford, and leave her?

"That's all? He just *left?*"

Claire was silent a moment, busy with her gears and her mirrors as she maneuvered around a double-parked car.

"Well, we talked for a moment. He said he knew you were very bitter, that you were liable to do something crazy. He said you were making the whole thing up, and I believed him."

"You had every right to," I told her.

She frowned, not looking at me. "No. I was very upset and I wasn't thinking. It wasn't until long after he was gone that I pulled myself together and called your father." The way she brushed aside what I said was beginning to bother me. She seemed to be interested in me only as a source of information.

After a moment she went on. "He said he didn't know what was happening, but he'd call me when you arrived. Twenty minutes later he did call and told me you'd been arrested. And then I knew. . . ." She broke off, shook her head. "I'm sorry I took so long to believe you and acted so slowly once I did."

It was a typical Claire Cowan speech, graceful and reserved. She was not interested in my apologies but felt she had to make her own. It was all quite impersonal, a matter of duty to herself, not regard for me.

We came to a red light and stopped. Her hands dropped into her lap, nervously rubbing little circles on her knees. Then she realized that I was watching her and quickly put them back on the wheel.

I felt sick at heart. I realized that this day had been very cruel to Claire, and she was trying to hide all her worry and pain from me—the shock of my accusations; Wimpy Jim's quick withdrawal from the scene, leaving her alone; the call to my father; the long, anxious wait; and his call, with the news of my arrest. Then there was the swift, unavoidable conclusion that Jim had turned me in, the realization of all he was hiding from her.

My anger turned away from her, toward myself. Why hadn't I seen through her coolness? It had always been a point of honor with Claire to hide her worries; she had not spoken of the problems of her parents until I saw them for myself. Even now she acted in character.

I had to break down her reserve, and I turned to her and spoke, choosing my words carefully. "You must have realized as soon as he left you alone that something was wrong."

But she was watching the road. The light had changed and we started off.

"How do you mean?"

"Well, you were upset, and he didn't stay with you. . . ." I stopped, seeing her mouth set coldly.

"Not really. Jim's a very pleasant guy. He's never known how to deal with unpleasant situations."

I leaned toward her, and she seemed almost physically to draw away from me.

"Claire, do you have any idea how he got involved in this drug thing in the first place?"

"No." Her lips closed tight on the word.

"But surely—he's your boyfriend—you must have—"

She interrupted. "You must understand that a romance between an aspiring lawyer and an aspiring doctor is a pretty rushed affair. We see each other only over coffee during study breaks. So I can't really answer your question."

The flipness of her reply took my breath away. Did

she really care so little for him? No, I thought at once bitterly, she cares so little for me. She doesn't want to discuss her personal life with me, wants to cut me off as coldly as she can. I turned away from her and looked out the windshield.

We were just turning onto Forty-second Street.

"What are we doing *here*?" I saw the imposing mass of the station only a block away.

"We have to get the—the boxes before we go up to Hartford, of course."

I looked at the line of yellow taxis and remembered the police car parked there, the wire screen and locked doors, the handcuffs, the curious faces of the crowd.

"No, I can't go back in there."

We were crossing Lexington Avenue. Claire put on her signal to pull over. "We have to have the boxes with us."

I thought of Tony's men: Suppose one of them was still around, patiently watching the locker? Right now I was safe, but if I were seen . . .

"No," I said. "We can't because—"

And then she turned angrily on me.

"Look, Arthur, we're going to do what I say now. This doesn't even concern you any more. It's my problem, and I'll handle it my way."

I stared at her in silence. Now it was coming out; I wanted to hear everything.

"You've made a mess of this whole business. You grabbed those packages and sat on them. You weren't interested in the truth. You just wanted to torment me and your father. Well, you were dead wrong!"

She flung open her door. "And now it's my problem. Give me the key, and I'll get the damned things."

She held out her hand, and I gave it to her. Then she got out and ran to the station, her raincoat flapping behind her, and disappeared through the long row of glass doors.

I leaned over and pulled her door shut. She thought

of me as an enemy, a bumbling enemy blinded by his own suspicions and vindictiveness. Very well, I would let her handle this if she wanted. I would not tell her about Tony or about the girl. I had dangers of my own to avoid, and I must be careful how I used Claire, what I told her, and what I left out.

Right now it suited my purposes that she go to the locker. Tony's man had never seen her, and surely he would not remember which one of the lockers I had gone to.

In fact I was wrong about that, as I was wrong about everything. Tony's man did remember. But I did not see him as I scanned the station doors after Claire walked out with the boxes in her arms, and I did not see the car that followed us to Hartford. I did not know until it was too late.

12

It was nightfall by the time we reached Hartford's northwestern suburbs. The rain clouds seemed to have sunk under their own weight and now lay along the western horizon in banks as purplish-blue and substantial as a distant mountain range. I looked up and watched the light and color drain from the clear sky overhead.

The drive had been long and grim. Claire had not spoken a word to me, and I had looked out the window and listened to the grind and rattle of the engine as she fought her way through the Friday afternoon rush on 95. I remembered the efforts and anticipation I had gone through in the old days to speak to her on the phone for just five minutes. I would never have believed that I could spend three hours beside her and find nothing at all to say.

We topped a hill, and I caught a glimpse of Wentworth Hospital's towers through dusk and trees, and then we turned off onto a side road.

Jim lived in a new apartment court, a pair of three-story shoe boxes facing each other across a parking lot. They were made of beige brick; one building had paneling of green plastic above the door, the other, yellow plastic. A floodlit sign at the entrance tried to convince you this was Avon Gardens despite the lack of floral evidence.

We splashed through a few potholes and parked before the green-plastic building. Claire switched off the engine and twisted around to pick up the two cartons in the back seat. She tucked them under her arm and got out. She had not looked inside them.

We went in and walked up a flight of stairs to a corridor with pebbly plastered walls and an all-weather carpet. Claire stopped at a tan steel door and lifted a miniature brass knocker. A muted two-tone chime sounded inside.

I glanced at her as she dropped her hand and put it back in the pocket of her raincoat. Her head was bowed and turned away, her face hidden behind the curtain of her hair. She was looking at the boxes, and I wondered what she was thinking.

"Come in," called a voice. Claire seemed not to hear, so I opened the door and walked in.

It was a long, narrow room, furnished with the usual collection of scarred tables and threadbare couches, but against one wall stood a sumptuous green leather recliner chair. I knew that must be Jim's; he craved comfort like an old cat.

At the moment the room was empty but for the low, mellow voice of Gordon Lightfoot coming out of the stereo speakers, singing, "If You Could Read My Mind." Claire hesitated by the door, as if she wanted to slip quietly out. I advanced into the room and shouted, "Anybody home?" I wanted very much to talk to Wimpy, even if Claire didn't.

A short, pleasant-looking young man in a white coat leaned around the angle of the wall. He saw Claire and smiled.

"Oh, Claire. Hi."

She still stood by the door. "Is Jim at the hospital?" she asked hopefully.

"No, he's right here. Come on in." He disappeared around the corner.

For another moment she hesitated. The corners of her mouth tightened and a single deep cleft of con-

centration settled between her eyebrows. Abruptly she
decided. She put the boxes on the floor, turned to
lock the door, and quickly walked past me across the
room.

I followed her into the kitchen. Jim sat with his back
to us at a small table against the wall, his broad
shoulders hunched and tense under his white coat, his
massive head bowed over the table. For a wild moment I thought he must be in a state of nervous ex-
haustion, about to burst into sobs the moment he saw
us. Then I perceived that he was looking with rapt
attention at something before him on the table. The
roommate, who had a black shield on his chest that
read FRED RICHMOND, M.D., sat across from him. As
we approached, he grinned and put a finger to his
lips, directing us to be silent.

I stepped around and saw that Jim held a light
plastic ashtray in his large right hand. With infinite
calculation, he drew it back and, flipping his wrist,
flung it across the table. It slid toward the opposite
side, slowed, hung balanced for a moment on the edge,
and then toppled into Fred's lap.

"Damn," said Jim, straightening up as Fred laughed.
And then, finally, he looked up at us, his smile flashing
brilliantly in his dark beard.

"Ah, Claire, Mr. Lavien, so glad to see you. I need
someone to cheer me on. Fred is killing me in the ashtray sweepstakes here."

His welcoming smile faded the moment he stopped
speaking, and he turned quickly away from us. I felt
sure he had prepared a lengthy flippant routine to
protect himself from us, but now he didn't have the
heart to bring it off.

"Jim—" Claire said softly.

He reacted as if he had been touched with a lash,
and started talking quickly.

"It's a game of consummate skill, isn't it, Fred?"

"Absolutely," Fred agreed, still grinning.

"The object is to slide this ashtray across this highly polished surface—"

"Hours of work went into the surface," interjected Fred.

"—and get it as close as possible to the edge without sending it over. Fred has given up medicine completely to practice—"

Fred denied this.

"—and can now, at will, hang it out exactly at the balancing point."

Fred told him to show us the balancing point.

"Yes. This major-league-approved ashtray has a red mark, as you can see, exactly at the balancing point, which Fred invariably lines up with the end of the table."

He held the ashtray up to us, and as he did so, his eyes met Claire's. That was fatal. He had been doing quite well up to then; but as he looked into those blue eyes, narrowed with apprehension and sadness, his nerve broke. He put the ashtray down on the table and looked away. His shoulders sagged heavily, and he could think of no more to say.

"Jim, I have to talk to you."

Again he winced at the sound of Claire's voice. He stood up.

"Sure, but I've got to do the dishes first. It's my turn, and Fred will let them rot before he'll do them, right, Fred?"

"They can wait," said Claire softly.

"It's O.K. I'll do them," Fred put in quickly. I glanced at him, and he raised his eyebrows knowingly. No doubt he thought Claire and Jim were having a lovers' quarrel or a minor altercation about what they would do next weekend.

They didn't look at each other. They stood, oddly, in the same posture, heads bowed and hands in their pockets.

"We'll—uh—we'll go to my room," said Jim at length.

Fred motioned to the empty chair across the table. "Care to challenge the defending champ, uh—Mr. Levine?"

It was a tactful move, and both Jim and Claire glanced at me, hoping I would agree to it.

But this was no lovers' quarrel. Wimpy had tried to put me in jail, and I wasn't about to leave him to Claire's merciful hands. "No, thanks," I said. "Let's go."

Jim stepped out into the living room, hesitated, and went to turn off the record player. Then he turned and saw Claire picking up the boxes from the floor. Although his expression was hidden by the dark-framed glasses and the thick, inscrutable beard, I could see a flush spreading across his cheeks. Without looking at him she went down the hallway to his room. He turned and looked blankly at me for a moment, then followed her.

He turned into his room and sat on the edge of an enormous double bed. Claire turned his desk chair around and sat down facing him. She dropped the boxes on the bed. He turned away like an animal shying from a sudden movement, and stood up.

"I've, uh—got to get some cigarettes," he mumbled and went out past me without looking up.

I pushed an anatomy book out of the way and sat down on the desk. I looked down at Claire, but again she turned her head away.

Jim returned, pulling a cigarette out of a pack. He had seen a few cancerous lungs in his time, and he bought a brand the filter of which was an elaborate construction of plastic and fiber guaranteed to cut down on nicotine. He smoked like some sort of pump, pulling the smoke into his mouth and instantly blowing it all out.

He peered at Claire but avoided her direct gaze.

Suddenly she leaned forward and spoke with an attempt at lightness.

"Is there anything else you'd like?"

Jim's lips twitched as he tried to grin, but all the banter had drained out of him. I suppose it was the first time he had ever let a joke of Claire's fall.

They both looked at the floor a moment, and Claire began reluctantly.

"Jim, we know you used my car on Wednesday night."

"Yes," he replied. "I did."

Then they just sat in silence, their heads bent close together, not looking at each other. Claire did not seem to know what to say next. I did.

"Don't you have anything you'd like to ask us, Jim?" I said sarcastically. They both looked up at me. "Like why I'm not in jail right now despite your best efforts to put me there?"

"I—I don't really know what's going on," he said pitifully.

I stood up. "Look, Wimpy, for Christ's sake—"

"Arthur, be quiet!" Claire's voice remained low and even, but there was a harsh edge to it, and as she turned to face me, she held her head very carefully erect, as if she were in pain. Again I felt sorry for her, and sat down.

She turned back; and now, finally, Jim looked at her pleadingly, hoping she would let him off the hook. Then she spoke, softly but forcefully.

"Jim, Arthur thought that I was driving the car Wednesday night. He thought these"—she put her hand on the boxes, but he did not look at them—"were supposed to go to his father."

Abruptly Jim looked up at me, ignoring Claire.

"The old bastard."

"What?"

"At Claire's you said, 'I'm going to dump these on the old bastard's desk.' You meant your father?"

I nodded, and he looked down, thinking, as if this bit of information was very important to him. He was really in bad shape. "But I never got there, because you called the cops, remember?" He did not look up. "And they nailed me. It would have worked perfectly, Wimpy, except that Claire and my father got me off."

Jim did not seem very interested in that now. And as I watched his stricken features, I suddenly wasn't angry at him any more. The expression of worry and fear on his handsome, pleasant face fitted him so poorly—he looked like a six-year-old at a funeral.

Jim stood, unexpectedly, and his knees bumped against Claire's.

"Sorry," he mumbled, stood, and walked away toward the window. After a moment he turned and took a deep, grateful breath, like a swimmer coming up for air.

"O.K.," he said. "I called the cops. I'm really sorry. I panicked and—" He broke off, took another breath. "It was stupid, and I'm really sorry. That's all."

Claire's shoulders relaxed, and she looked up at him. "Tell us everything, Jim. From the beginning."

Jim gave a fleeting, bitter smile. "The beginning?"

Claire leaned toward him, prompting him. "On Wednesday, remember, you were supposed to go home with Dad, and we meant to meet there and go back to the city together." She paused a moment, thinking. "But at three you called and told me you would have to go down to the city early—"

"Yes," said Jim. "O.K. I'll tell you all about it."

But as he came to sit down on the bed, something tugged my attention away, something in what Claire had just said didn't fit. But I shrugged it off and looked at Jim. Now we would get the truth from him, and no doubt he would cover what was bothering me.

"I had to run an errand while I was down in New York—had to deliver some papers to Dr. Sloane, in Greenwich. Anyway, I was telling one of the nurses in surgery about it, and she asked me if I'd do her a favor, since I was going down to the city anyway."

I could almost hear the click as it fell into place. I leaned forward.

"This nurse—she's a very pretty girl, about my age, tall, long blonde hair—right?"

They both stared up at me. Claire looked surprised, Wimpy looked ill.

"Yes," he said.

"What's her name?"

I expected him to refuse to tell me, but when Wimpy gave in, he gave in all the way.

"Angela. Angela Riles."

"You've seen this girl, Arthur?" Claire asked.

I didn't take my eyes off Jim. "She came to see me on Thursday morning. Jim told her where to find me. She begged me to give her the shit. She's a junkie."

He jumped up and stared at me wildly. For a moment I thought he would hurl himself through the window or swing at me. But no; he only stood wavering for a moment, and then said, "I have to go to the bathroom."

I felt like laughing. Claire said sharply, "Jim, there's only one way out of this—you've got to tell us the truth. Don't you understand? You're helping an addict get drugs. You can go to prison for what you've done."

That hit him hard, and he slumped into a chair. "But I've done nothing wrong!" he whined.

Claire was silent for a moment, then she said quietly, "I hope—I'm sure—you didn't mean to, but you have done something very wrong."

He stared morosely at the floor and seemed to forget that we were even there.

Claire prompted him again. "This nurse—Angela—what did she want you to do for her?"

He answered without looking up. "She told me to deliver that box to a doctor in White Plains."

Claire and I stared at each other.

"*She* gave you those boxes?"

He raised his head and looked for the first time at the two packages on the bed.

"One box. She gave me only one box."

Again Claire swung around to look at me. I shook my head. "He's lying."

Jim was staring at the floor again. He seemed not to have heard me, as if he were lost in dark and treacherous memories.

Claire was watching me intently. "Arthur, what exactly did you see on Wednesday night?"

"I saw a car park next to yours, and a kid got out and carried two packages over and dumped them in your car."

"You're sure he had *two* packages?"

I closed my eyes, trying to fight my way back through the tattered veils of my theories, back to the beginning. I pictured the road in Greenwich, the kid running in front of his car. It was dark and I was far away. Only from his posture could I tell that he was carrying something. I did not see the boxes until—

Yes. I had been wrong from the very beginning, wrong about everything.

I opened my eyes and looked at Claire. "When I got close enough to see, the kid was leaning into your car. The door was open and the light on, and I could see one package on the seat." I sighed miserably and finished. "I thought he'd just put it down, but it might have been there all the time."

"And the other package was in his hand?"

"Yes."

"So what you saw wasn't a drop—it was an exchange."

She had shaken off her fatigue, her tension. She seemed to tremble with excitement and relief. Claire had always believed that if you thought a problem through and reached the truth, all the pain and difficulties would disappear.

"An exchange?" I said.

She nodded. "Think. This girl is a nurse. She has a heroin habit. She can't get heroin in a hospital, and surely she can't pay for it."

I understand now. "You figure she's found a way to steal barbiturates from the hospital, and she's exchanging them for heroin?"

Again Claire nodded. Her eyes were shining. "What else can it be?"

I looked past her, at Jim. His head was up; he was listening now, and a smile of relief lurked at the corners of his mouth.

"And where do you fit into this?" I asked him. "How much did Angela tell you?"

His broad shoulders lifted in a helpless shrug. "Nothing. I've told you everything I know. I was to deliver the package to Dr. Bergson, in White Plains. But first I had these papers to take to Dr. Sloane, in Greenwich, and when I came out of his place, the box was gone."

Claire was facing him now. They exchanged a clear, untroubled look.

"You knew nothing at all about this exchange," Claire assured him. "The nurse knew you would be in Dr. Sloane's house, and she told the pusher where to find your car and what to do."

"Yes," said Jim happily. "I knew—I knew nothing about it."

I wasn't going to let him off so easily.

"So who is this Dr. Bergson you were supposed to take the box to?"

Claire spun around; she was ready for that. "I know him. He's a friend of our family's. And I know he's been away in Florida all this month. His house is empty." She turned to Jim again. "Don't you see? It was all carefully planned: these boxes are identical; that kid Arthur saw was going to switch them—take the pills and leave the heroin. Then you were to go on to Dr. Bergson's, find nobody home, and bring the heroin back to this nurse. She used you. You didn't know what you were doing."

He nodded his head slowly. "Right," he said, and he straightened up with an air of self-vindication and reached for a cigarette.

While he and Claire beamed at each other, I stood and came a step closer.

"Well, Jim, I'm glad to hear you're so innocent. So why, when you finally found out what was in those boxes, did you call the cops and try to frame me?"

His whole passive frame seemed to sag. He dropped the cigarette and got miserably to his feet.

"Look, I told you, I'm sorry I made that call. But I didn't know what was going on, and the way you came in threatening Claire scared the hell out of me. I panicked, that's all."

Claire turned to me, and her sunny confidence was gone now. "Arthur," she said desperately, "I can understand what he's saying—the way you acted, the shock of finding out what was in those boxes . . . Of course, there's no excuse—"

"Claire, just think, will you? He started lying when I wasn't around—when he says he didn't know what was in the boxes. On Wednesday night you came home and told him I'd seen your car in Greenwich, and he said he knew nothing about it."

She squinted and looked away, as if I had shone a bright light in her face.

"I don't believe any of this crap about Dr. Bergson or switching the boxes. He knew what he was doing, he's lied all along, and he's lying now."

She stood tiredly and addressed him without looking at him.

"Jim, has this girl got some—some hold over you?"

Then he did something that surprised us. He went to the bed, tore open the flaps of one of the boxes, and stared in at the light-blue capsules.

"It's Amytal," I told him sarcastically. I was getting tired of him.

He nodded and tossed the box aside, then opened the other one. He took out one of the plastic bags and examined it.

"Heroin," I said.

He shook some of the white powder into his hand. "No," he said, "it's morphine." He stared down at it and for a long time was silent. "She's on morphine," he said in a hushed voice.

"That doesn't matter, Jim," said Claire pleadingly. "You're still supplying an addict, and you have to tell us why, or we can't help you."

Slowly he raised his head and looked at her, and I knew, suddenly, what he was holding back. I knew, too, that he could not possibly tell Claire.

He folded up the bag and dropped it back in the box. "Claire," he said, "don't go any further with this, please." His voice was steady, as if he had given up all hope for himself and cared about nothing but sparing her the pain of finding it all out.

"It's too late now. I have to know. If you don't tell me, I'll have to find the girl."

Jim got up and walked away to the window, turning his back on us.

"I won't tell you anything more."

I looked at Claire. She backed away a step; she knew that he was not just confused and frightened now. He seemed to have understood at last what he had done, and it horrified him. She stared at his back for a moment, then abruptly turned and walked out the door.

I picked up the boxes and followed, leaving Jim standing in silence at the window.

I caught up with her in the lobby. She had paused with her hand on the knob, not knowing where to go next. I hurried down the steps and stopped close behind her. I would have to tell her what Jim could not, and I didn't know how to do it.

"Claire, he really does care for you," I began clumsily.

"If he cared for me, he would have trusted me."

I stared blankly at the little row of brass mailboxes on the wall and tried to think of a way to begin. When I turned back, she was facing me, with narrowed, suspicious eyes.

"You know," she said stonily. "You know what he's hiding."

I nodded. "He's—he's helping her steal the pills."

I watched her, wishing that she would burst into tears or strike at me or do anything. But she only looked away, considered, and shook her head.

"No, you can't be sure of that. She could be doing it on her own." Her disbelief was almost contemptuous.

"Claire, I know he's helping her."

She gave me a hard look. "Why would he do that?"

"Because he's her lover."

She didn't flinch. She only looked at me for a moment as if wondering why I should tell her such stupid and ugly lies.

"That can't be. I would know."

She was forcing me to do this in the cruelest way. "I'm sorry," I said, "but I'm telling you the truth. Angela admitted it to me."

"When?" she asked at once.

"Yesterday, but I didn't know until now that—that she meant Jim."

Claire turned and went out the door.

Outside the clouds had drifted back, to cast a grey pall over the night sky, and there was a wet, chill wind. Claire walked briskly ahead of me to the car, her hands stuffed into the pockets of her raincoat. Her slim, bare legs looked frail in the sensible, heavy moccasins she wore. When we reached the Volvo, she didn't get in but stood with her back turned and head bowed.

I opened the car door and put the packages in the back seat, and then some instinct made me straighten up and look around, searching the shadows of the parking lot.

It took me a moment to realize that I was looking for Tony's men. I tried to tell myself that I was safe, that I had lost them in New York. But then I thought, Tony must know that Angela is a nurse at Wentworth. He could be in Hartford right now. And the kid with the knife knew Claire's Volvo. The wind blew up, and I shivered. Tonight was the deadline. If he found me with the drugs now . . .

I wanted to get it over with, get rid of those two packages. I looked at Claire across the roof of the car. "Claire, we have to go to the police now. Turn it over to them."

She pulled the keys out of her pocket and began sorting through them.

"No. Not yet."

"But we know everything we—"

"Do we? Do you think I believe you?"

I stared at her in shocked silence. It was not only her words but the way she had spoken them. Her voice, until now so low and even, was loud and harsh and bitter.

"You think that I'm lying to you?"

"Why shouldn't I? You started this thing to get your father and me. You wanted to put us both in prison. It must have been a real disappointment to you to find out that we were innocent. So now you want to get Jim. You have as much reason to hate him as either of us."

I looked at the ground. I could not be angry with her. She had every reason to think that of me.

"Look," I said. "You've got it wrong. There's something I haven't told you. The pusher, when he came to see me on Wednesday, he told me he had to have those pills by tonight. He said he'd kill me if I didn't give them to him."

Claire was silent, and after a moment I looked up at her.

She shrugged her shoulders and opened the car door. "You can't expect me to believe that. If this man really did come to see you, if he really had threatened you, you would have given him the boxes. I know you hate us, but you don't want to get your father and me badly enough to risk getting killed for it."

She got in the car. "We're going to Wentworth. I want to find this girl Angela."

I stood by the car, too miserable to move. I deserved this. I had treated her with hatred and mistrust, and I could not blame her for treating me the same way. I had tried to use those boxes as weapons, acting out of despair and envy. I had been wrong, and now it was too late to change. I remembered leaving my father's apartment only yesterday morning, when everything had seemed so simple. I was going to get the old bastard and die.

I knew how I had intended to take revenge, but how had I intended to die? I looked at that figure of myself, coming down in the elevator with the key in my pocket and the courage of despair in my heart. I had thought that my life was such a failure that it would somehow have to end.

It didn't work that way. I had not had the guts to end it myself on Wednesday night; instead, I had started this thing, this botched job of malice and stupidity, that was ending up as yet another duet of torture between Claire and me.

"Let's go, Arthur," she said impatiently, and I got into the car. We made the short drive to Wentworth in silence, not looking at each other.

13

Against the cloudy night sky the two towers of Wentworth Memorial Hospital stood out as patchworks of dark cement and lighted windows.

Wentworth had moved to this expensive hilltop in the suburbs a decade ago, and each year new wings and parking lots laid claim to the surrounding acreage. I remembered the hierarchy of these parking lots well: you drove through the doctors' lot, so close to the main building that the lights of the entrance were reflected on the hoods of the Cadillacs, then through the staff lot, and finally you reached the great, black asphalt desert of the visitors' lot, where a white gate dropped to bar your way. Visitors had to pay.

Claire took the time slip, and the gate bobbed up. She pulled into a space, and we left the car and made the long walk back to the main building. She stayed a step ahead of me to keep me out of her sight.

Entering Wentworth you walked through corridors with floors of flecked tile and soundproofed walls, as anonymous as an airport terminal. It was still visiting hour, and all around us were bald-headed men in corduroy coats and women whose bottoms drooped heavily in knitted pantsuits. Hospitals are always full of the middle-aged children of dying old people.

At the information desk was one of Wentworth's token blacks, a pretty young woman who gave Claire a broad smile.

"Hello, Miss Cowan."

Claire read her nameplate without seeming to. "Hello, Miss Jonas."

"I'm afraid Dr. Cowan's gone home for the evening."

Claire nodded and said that was all right, that she wanted to know where she could find Angela Riles.

"Is she on the staff here?"

"She's a nurse."

Miss Jonas nodded and pulled a directory from a bottom shelf. "Do you happen to know what division she's in at present?"

Claire shrugged helplessly, but I remembered that Jim had told us.

"She's in surgery."

Miss Jonas thumbed through the pages and found the name. "Yes, one of the post-op recovery wards— fifth floor."

Claire nodded and turned to the elevators. Miss Jonas offered to call the fifth floor, but she did not respond.

I received a shock as the elevator doors slid open. I remembered these recovery wards so well. Wentworth's interior decorators felt that if they made the hospital look like a motel, the patients might forget that they were sick. The corridors were papered in a frenetic floral print; and looking into the rooms you saw desks, easy chairs, and bright draperies. Only the glimpses of pale, bare limbs sprawled across beds, nurses carrying syringes and pills, and the urgent beeping of the cardiac monitors reminded you of the indignities of sickness.

The nurses' station was a broad L-shaped counter, surrounding blocks of filing cabinets and tables cluttered with folders and clipboards. We could see the white-capped heads of nurses bobbing above the cabinets, and at the nearest table a solitary resident ate his dinner off a tray.

He did not notice us, and for a moment we stood in silence at the counter. My head was stuffy with lack of sleep, and my stomach felt hollow and aching. But I did not want to lie down or to eat; I did not want to do anything.

I knew we would not find Angela. By now she was desperate for a shot; wherever she was tonight, she would not be capable of working. I remembered her lovely face and the way it had clouded with terror, and I wished fervently that I had given her the boxes when she'd asked for them, or at least given her enough dope for one lousy shot.

I wondered if Claire really wanted to see Angela, wondered what she was thinking now. I glanced at her. She was looking straight ahead, and the broad face with its wide-set blue eyes was utterly expressionless.

She addressed the resident in a clear voice. "Doctor?"

He turned around, dabbing at his mouth with a napkin. He was young, dark-haired, and wore wire-rimmed glasses.

"May I help you?"

"I'd like to speak to—to the head nurse on this floor."

"Barbara!" The doctor called and returned to his tray.

A middle-aged woman in white stepped out from behind one of the filing cabinets and came up to the counter. Her eyes and hair were the same shade of dull grey, and there were lines around her mouth that gave her an apprehensive look.

"Yes? May I help you?"

"I'm looking for a nurse who works on this floor. Angela Riles. Is she here?"

"Not right now, no." The nurse looked at Claire, and her eyes narrowed. "Are you a friend of hers?"

"No, I'm—" Claire broke off, thought a moment. "I'm Claire Cowan. Dr. Cowan's daughter."

"Oh!" The nurse's hand fluttered to her mouth. There was a gold wedding ring a quarter of an inch wide on her worn finger. "Then Dr. Cowan did get my message?"

"Has something happened to her?" Claire asked tensely.

"Oh, no, nothing that we know of. Only she hasn't reported for work the last two days or called in. I tried to reach her, but she's not at home either." She frowned and hurried on. "I called your father's secretary yesterday morning, but he never got back to me. I know he's very busy, and I didn't want to make an official report, before talking to him—I mean, it could be nothing. And since we've had enough staff to cover . . ."

She began to describe to us her struggles in arranging the shifts to make up for Angela's absence. After a moment, Claire interrupted.

"Was she here on Wednesday night?"

"No, she works days." The nurse paused, thought again. "No, I'm sorry, on Wednesday afternoon Joan Wexler called in sick and Angela had to work the evening shift, too." She began to explain to us why it was necessary to put Angela on this shift; she seemed frightened that Claire would report unfavorably about her to her father.

I glanced at Claire. Now we knew why Angela had turned to Jim: she could not go down to New York and make the exchange herself.

Again Claire broke in on the nurse's ramblings. "Can you remember, did Angela have to make a lot of phone calls when you told her she had to work?"

The nurse looked at her, startled. "Why, yes." She nodded vigorously, and her voice became even more hurried and anxious. "She kept going to the pay phone, too. She wouldn't use the one on the desk."

No, Angela would not have wanted anyone to overhear her calls to Jim and to Tony, arranging the exchange.

"I suppose you'll want to call your father now," the nurse went on. "If he wants to talk to me . . ."

I looked at Claire. This had never occurred to us,

and for a moment it sounded so inviting. Tom was Chief of Surgery, after all. He would know what to do, whom to talk to. We could call him and wait here until the matter—and the boxes—were in official hands. I would be safe from Tony.

"No," said Claire firmly. "I think you're right not to bother him. This can wait awhile. Thanks for your help."

With an effort she put on a reassuring smile. But even as the nurse started to reply, Claire had turned and started back down the hall.

She walked with long, swift strides, and I did not catch up with her until she stood at the elevator, pressing the call button.

"Claire," I said, "wouldn't it be better if—"

Still she would not look at me. "If we call my father, he'll go to the police immediately. What else could he do?"

"What else can *we* do, now?"

She took a shallow breath and said, "I'm going to see a friend of my father's, in the pharmacy. Maybe I can find out how Angela is stealing the pills."

Or how Jim is helping her do it, I thought. The doors slid open, and she stepped in and turned, sagging tiredly against the wall, head bowed and hands once again in the pockets of her raincoat. For a moment I could see her face and realized why she had turned away so abruptly from both the nurse and Miss Jonas. She could hold her pose of calm authority only for a short time. Now she looked exhausted and worried and dejected. She knew it was all no good.

I got in and stood beside her as the doors closed. "Claire, why do you have to go on with this? If Jim's innocent, if he didn't know what was in those boxes, he's got nothing to fear from the police. And if—"

I broke off, but she knew what I was thinking.

"If he's guilty, there's nothing I can do," she said

flatly. She sighed and rubbed her forehead. "Why don't you just keep quiet, Arthur? If you're right, you can watch me get the evidence to put Jim in prison. You should enjoy that."

There was no anger in her voice now, only a harsh, defeated bitterness that made me feel cold inside. She knew that I was right, and I wondered why she kept on going, why she took all this upon herself. I looked at the clear, strong lines of her profile and the set of her large head on the thin, almost frail shoulders, and slowly I began to understand. Or rather, to remember.

It had taken me a long time to figure out Claire's proud, shy character. When we met, my life was so much broader than hers, a busy round of committee meetings, late nights at the school paper, and, before the tennis season began, long dope-smoking parties. And yet she had a confidence and self-sufficiency that I had never attained. I did not understand it until the next year, when the naïve political optimism on which I had staked my all had fallen and taken me down with it, while she moved from one success to another at Radcliffe. It was as if she had thought her life out in advance, and now it was all coming to pass according to plan.

She had, in fact, done just that. In her lonely adolescence she had come to understand that her parents had failed her and themselves—one was too bitter, and the other too preoccupied, ever to set things right. Without blaming them, she had retreated from them and taken the responsibility for her life upon herself. Since there was no one around to help her, it had become necessary for her to believe that she could do anything if she thought it out and made an effort.

As we had grown apart in our freshman year, my only comfort was the knowledge that her confidence was based on an illusion, that there were situations which could not be made to come out all right no matter how much intelligence and care she brought to bear on them. With the malice born of envy, I waited for her to fail.

Now it was going to happen. This visit to her father's friend would do her no good, and she would have to go to the police. She would draw on all her invention and courage, and it would do her no good. I had done this to her, and she was right to blame me for it.

The elevator doors opened.

We were in the entrails of the hospital now, a long corridor with rough cinder-block walls and rows of thick pipes running along the ceiling, in and out of the circles of light cast by intermittently spaced bare bulbs. I followed Claire down to a pair of glass doors with PHARMACY printed on them. As we went in, she took her hands out of her pockets and squared her shoulders. Her voice was brisk and purposeful as she addressed a man in a lab coat behind the counter.

"Good evening. Is Mr. Van Brocken in?"

The man nodded. "You're in luck. He's still in his office."

"Thank you," she said, and stepped around the counter to knock on a door marked PRIVATE.

"Yes?"

"It's Claire Cowan, Mr. Van Brocken."

"Claire!" said the muffled voice with pleasure. We heard steps, and the door opened.

Van Brocken was probably under forty, but overweight had made him prematurely old. Behind his glasses, small dark eyes rested on little sacks of fat, and there was no trace of a jawbone between his thick neck and sagging cheeks.

Beaming at Claire, he took her hand in both of his. "Well, this is a pleasure! We don't see much of you these days."

She smiled and said it was good to see him. She told him what she was doing, giving the impression that living in New York was a terrible deprivation because it kept her so far from Wentworth. Then she listened patiently as he talked about Tom, and managed to nod and smile when he mentioned having lunch with Jim the week before.

It would have taken a much more alert observer than Van Brocken to notice that her wide blue eyes, usually so calm and level in their gaze, were wandering sightlessly around the room, and that the hands folded in front of her were shaking slightly.

Presently she said, with just the right amount of shyness, "Actually, Mr. Van Brocken, I came to see you because I need a little expert advice."

"Oh, I see," he said, and his smile broadened. He liked that.

She explained very convincingly that Maitland, Ruthven was doing work on drug laws for the state and that she had been asked to write a report on leaks from hospitals and pharmacies. She finished by introducing me as a colleague from Maitland, Ruthven.

I was surprised by the elaborateness of all this. Claire obviously did not want to alarm Van Brocken as she had Angela's supervisor. But I wondered how she could think it all through clearly and how she had the heart to carry it out.

Van Brocken accepted the story. Fortunately he did not know that Maitland, Ruthven had not a trace of social consciousness to its name, and he frowned and nodded solemnly, and invited us to sit down.

We took two plain straight-backed chairs before the green metal desk, and he sat in his chair, beneath his framed degrees in pharmacology.

"This, of course, is a serious problem," he began, "but more in hospitals in the city than for us." He smugly told us stories of drug robberies at Mt. Sinai. Claire sat through it patiently; she even got out a pad and pretended to take notes. I could see her hand form cramped, awkward letters on the page. Slowly she narrowed the discussion to barbiturates, and to Wentworth.

"I understand that a lot of these drug robberies are—are inside jobs." Van Brocken nodded solemnly, and Claire went on, watching his face for any sign that she was hitting home. "Would it be possible for someone on staff to slowly pilfer a large supply of pills?"

He shook his head imperturbably and started to fill a pipe.

"Impossible."

"But surely there are large supplies of sleeping pills and tranquilizers in many places—"

"Oh, yes. At the nurses' stations in every ward, and many of the doctors keep supplies in their consulting rooms." He jabbed the air emphatically with his unlit pipe. "But every drug that comes into the hospital goes through this pharmacy, and we keep careful records. We have to—the Government is very strict." He stuck the pipe in his mouth and lit it. Squinting at Claire through the rising smoke he asked, "Would it help you to know the procedures?"

When she did not respond, I glanced at her. Her head was down, and she had given up the pretext of taking notes. Her control was beginning to go. After a moment she said listlessly, "Please."

"We keep records here of everything that comes into the hospital"—he jerked the pipe stem at rows of green filing cabinets along one wall of the office—"and where it goes to. And the doctors and nurses on each floor have to account for everything they use."

The chair squeaked as he leaned back. "To take the example of a supply of drugs in a doctor's office," he began.

As he spoke I wondered what good this could possibly do us. Jim and Angela had obviously found some way to get the pills that had completely fooled Van Brocken; he could tell us nothing. I looked at Claire, waiting for her to interrupt. But she was staring at the floor. She knew she had nowhere to go from this room, and she did not want to leave.

Van Brocken was telling us about something called a Blue Book. "Now the FDA requires every physician who keeps drugs in his office to keep a Blue Book, covering all Grade II restricted drugs. In this book he has to note every time he issues a prescription—the date, the amount prescribed, and the name of the patient. Now we keep here a record of what quantity of each drug we issue to the doctors, and the FDA men come around every month and lay the Blue Books and our records side by side." He grinned, and his chins bobbed heavily. "And brother, the prescriptions issued and the drugs given out better match up, or there's hell to pay."

Again there was silence; again I glanced at Claire. She was staring at the wall above Van Brocken's head, and her face had the weary, defeated look again. I knew she was not listening any more, and I had better say something.

"So it's impossible for any kind of drug theft to go unnoticed."

He nodded and sucked on his pipe. "We have to account for every damned pill from the factory to the patient's mouth."

He rumbled out a laugh, and with an effort I laughed, too.

Then there was silence, and I stood up and looked at Claire. "Shall we go?" We were at a dead end now; we had to go to the police.

But she remained seated and looked dully at Van Brocken. "You have the same procedures at the nurses' stations?"

"Oh, yes. We would know immediately if there was a shortage."

"And there have been no leaks of drugs from this hospital at all?"

He nodded, rising heavily to his feet. He took Claire's arm as she got up and made a joke about being glad he could be so little help to her on this particular paper.

And then, with his hand on the doorknob, he hesitated.

"As a matter of fact, we did have a bad scare a couple of months ago, but it turned out to be nothing."

He stood oblivious in a cloud of pipe smoke, not noticing our eyes, our silence. After a moment he went on with a shrug.

"But that wasn't what you're interested in—that was morphine."

Morphine. The word jolted me, and at once I knew. Before turning to Tony, Angela had tried to get the stuff from here. Had Jim helped her with that, too?

"Was anyone caught?" The taut urgency of my voice frightened me.

But Van Brocken, incredibly, did not notice. He just shook his head, puffed on his pipe, and said, "Oh, no, it turned out to be nothing at all really. I don't know why I even brought it up."

"What happened?"

"Oh, I was going over the books from one of the wards when I noticed there were several ampules of morphine unaccounted for. Well, I called the chief of service involved—"

"You thought someone was pilfering them?"

"Not really. Of course, it was possible—the drugs at nurses' stations aren't really as secure as I'd like to see them—but I thought it was much more likely a paperwork error—you know, one of the nurses gave a patient an injection and forgot to write it up."

"Where—" Claire swallowed and began again. "Where did this happen?"

"I'm afraid the Board has a tiresome rule against giving out specific information in a case like this." And he put his pipe in his mouth, as if to seal his lips.

Claire raised her head and looked at him, and I will never forget her eyes. They even alarmed Van Brocken, and he snatched the pipe from his mouth and stared back at her.

She noticed, and with a supreme effort she forced a smile and said lightly, "I can ask my father."

He chuckled. "Well, you've seen through me. It *was* in surgery, one of the post-op recovery wards—the fifth floor, I think."

Angela's floor.

And then I knew. After so many stupid mistakes, so many lies, we had reached the end. At that moment it was not a matter of speculation or of evidence; I simply saw before me a face: a strong, handsome face with mournful, deep-set eyes.

"And, of course, it was your father I talked to about it."

"What did my father say?"

It seemed to me that there was a gulf of silence before Van Brocken answered, silence so intense that I could hear the hum of the electric clock on the wall.

"He said I was right. He checked with his people and found out it was a paperwork error."

Tom had known for months that Angela was an addict. He was covering up for her. He was getting the pills for her.

I remember nothing about our good-byes to Van Brocken or about leaving the pharmacy. The next thing I knew, we were in the corridor again. And swiftly, terribly, the rest of it fell into place.

Angela had no hold over Jim, but Tom did. The Chief of Surgery, his girlfriend's father, had called him on Wednesday night and said, "Would you mind going down to New York early and running a couple of errands for me?" Of course, he had agreed.

Now I recalled walking up to the Cowans' house on Wednesday night, and Tom at the door, calling out "Jim?" before he saw my face. He feared that something had gone wrong, and Jim had come back. Claire had been right about the plan to switch the boxes, and the phony errand to the empty house—Jim had had no idea what he was doing.

He had called Tom that night to tell him the box had been stolen from his car, and Tom had told him to keep quiet about it and nothing else. Then Jim knew that he had gotten himself into some kind of trouble, but he was too spineless to pull himself out of it. He did not know what was going on, but Tom did and told him what to do. He had obeyed.

Jim really had not known what was in the boxes until I told him this morning at Claire's. I remembered him staring at me only an hour ago and saying, "The old bastard—you mean your father?" In his fear and bewilderment, he had thought I intended to dump out the pills on Tom Cowan's desk and had called to warn him.

And Tom had called the police.

I remembered him offering me a beer, asking me about myself, telling me about his problems with his wife. And two days later he had turned me in to the police. How frightened he must have been—must be, right now.

All along, I had suspected Jim, who knew nothing except that he was in trouble, and it would get worse unless he protected Tom Cowan. Only when he opened the boxes and saw the morphine did he know what Tom was doing, and then, horrified, he had made one last attempt to spare Claire.

I turned to her and for a long moment we looked at each other. Then, desperately, she shook her head.

"We don't know—we can't be sure yet."

"Claire—"

"She could have lied to him about making a paper-work mistake with the morphine—and he believed her and told Van Brocken it was all right—and then she found an outside source, started stealing the pills in some way—"

I cut in on the hurried, frightened voice. "*He* found her the outside source, Claire. Remember Larry Preston? The guy who was so into drugs at Loomis?"

"Yes," she said vaguely.

"Your father remembered him. He sent Angela to him and Larry put her on to the morphine pusher."

Her eyes flashed round on me.

"You're sure of that?"

"Claire, you've got to stop now. There's nothing more you can do."

But already she had turned away to the elevator.

"We don't know that he's getting her the pills," she said in a voice hushed with fear and desperation. "That's the only thing that matters. And we've got to make sure."

14

Miss Jonas smiled pleasantly as we approached. "Did you find that nurse you wanted to see, Miss Cowan?"

Claire put her hand on the edge of the desk and stared down at it. "I have to go up to my father's office." She struggled with the next phrase for a moment, then said simply, "For papers . . . he needs."

"Surely," said Miss Jonas, and she raised her hand.

A security guard, a middle-aged man with a bad limp, walked up to the desk.

"Jack, will you take the young lady up to Dr. Cowan's office and unlock it for her?"

The man hesitated. "Gee, I don't know. You'll have to call the doctor."

She gave him a tolerant smile. "This is Dr. Cowan's daughter."

"Oh, sure. There's no problem then."

With a jerky movement, Claire turned away from the desk. Miss Jonas looked after her, her smile giving way to a puzzled expression.

"Thank you," I said loudly. She nodded to me, and I followed Claire and the guard to the elevator.

The doors opened, casting a square of light on the dark wall opposite. We walked down the hallway until we came to a broad oak door that read THOMAS COWAN, M.D., CHIEF OF SURGERY.

The guard pulled a heavy jingling ring of keys from his pocket, ran through them, found the right one, and opened the door. "O.K.," he said to me, "when you go out, just be sure to press the lock button on the inside here."

I thanked him, too, and followed Claire inside.

We crossed the dark waiting room and went through a door, down a short, narrow corridor to another door.

It was Cowan's office. She turned on the light and walked across the thick blue carpet to the desk, stood before it for a moment, then knelt stiffly and started to run through the drawers. I did not know what she was trying to do; I was too worn out to think. Again I wondered how she could go on.

She searched for a long time, while I stared blankly at the top of the desk. There was a blotter of the same blue as the carpet, and a matching leather pencil case and letter opener were lying beside a picture of Claire at fifteen or so, matted on a simple cardboard stand.

She shut the door with a thud that sounded startlingly loud in the quiet office, and got up and crossed the room. In her hand was a ring with two keys. I followed her down the hall into another room.

It was an ordinary consulting room, small, bare, and windowless with white tiled walls and, beside the examination table, a stand covered with bright steel cases and glittering instruments. On the wall was a Norman Rockwell print: a little boy stood in a doctor's office, his trousers down, staring nervously at the degrees framed on the wall as the white-haired doctor prepared to give him a shot.

In one corner stood a small metal cabinet. Claire knelt beside it, inserted the key, and opened the doors.

Inside the shelves were crammed with vials, ampules, and a few large, brown-tinted glass jars with plastic tops. Several were labeled AMYTAL, and they were all empty.

I thought, surely, that this would be the end. But in silence she shut the doors, got up, and walked back to the office.

Again she knelt by the desk and methodically began

trying each of the drawers. The bottom one on the left was locked, and she opened it with the second key on the ring.

I walked around beside her as she rose and placed a thick spiral notebook with a blue cover on the desk. There was a lot of white print on the front: *Issued by the Food and Drug Administration/Grade II Drugs—Restricted*. Below were lines of regulations and warnings.

She stared at it for a while, then turned and went into the outer office.

She stood before a wall of filing cabinets, looked at them for a long moment, then stepped forward and slid open the top one. She moved more and more lethargically as she checked each of the drawers, like a swimmer in cold water, as if she were fighting to conserve her strength.

She knelt beside one of the bottom files.

"These are the records on his current patients," she said slowly and softly. "Everyone he's now prescribing for should have a folder here, and—"

"I understand," I told her at once. I didn't want to force her to speak any more than was necessary. I returned to Tom's office and sat down before the Blue Book.

She was thinking clearly, right to the end. The FDA would check this book against the supplies of Amytal issued to Tom. In it he would have to account for all the pills he took. If Tom was taking large numbers of them for Angela, he could cover up only by entering prescriptions in the book to nonexistent patients. And these patients would not be listed in his own files.

I opened the book to blank pages and flipped back to last month. There were four columns on the page: the patient's name, the date, the drug, and the amount. I looked down the columns. On some pages every other listing read "Amytal." I wished I didn't have to do this, but there was no way out.

I picked a name from March 9.

"P. Mellors."

Across the silent office I could hear Claire pulling out a drawer, thumbing through the folders.

"Yes," she said tonelessly, "he's here."

"A. Johnson."

Again the pause, the small sounds as she shifted papers.

"Yes."

"B. Stieble."

The pause was longer this time.

"How—how do you spell it?"

I told her.

"No."

"J. Nester."

"No."

I gave her five more names, and she found only one. It was agony to sit in that expensive leather chair, calling names out across the large, quiet office and waiting for Claire's soft "no" from the darkness outside the door. Presently, in the long pauses while she searched, I began trying to find names that began with the same letter, frantically hunting through the pages out of some absurd hope that this would make it easier for her. At least those terrible pauses would be shorter.

"P. Morelli."

I could hear the dry ruffle of the papers.

"No."

"A. Morse."

"No."

"D. Mahan."

"No."

Finally I could bear it no longer, and I closed the book and put it away.

She was kneeling on the floor, her fingers splayed over the files in an open drawer. She heard me come into the room, and without turning she listlessly pushed the drawer closed, got up, and went out the door. I turned out the lights, set the lock, and followed her.

She stood by the elevator, pressing the call button. Then suddenly her arm fell, and she reeled toward the stair door, flung it open, and ran through. I hurried after her.

She had stopped on the first landing, and was crying.

I had never seen Claire cry; somehow I had expected that she would do it quietly and gracefully. But now she stood below me, a frail, white-coated figure in the dim stairwell, her face in her hands and her shoulders shaking as she wept in great, gulping sobs.

I ran down the stairs and stopped beside her. She was too miserable even to turn away. I reached out my arms to her, and then let them fall as I remembered what she thought of me.

After a long time her sobs abated, and she spoke in a broken whisper. "He's—he's so proud to be Chief of Surgery at Wentworth." She stopped, swallowed, and went on haltingly. "Nothing else in his life has turned out very well, but he—always had that. And now . . ."

She shuddered and fought down a sob, then jerked her hands away from her face. Her cheeks were flushed and wet with tears. Hurriedly I ran through my pockets. I didn't even have a handkerchief to give her.

I looked up to find her eyes on me. They were wide and startlingly blue through her tears. And they were full of horror.

"How did you come on that car in the first place?" Her voice, suddenly harsh, echoed down the stairs. "Why have you done this?"

I stared at her helplessly, guiltily. I had built a machine to destroy my father. I had made mistake after mistake, lost control, and the mechanism hummed smoothly on, unable to be stopped.

But then Claire took her eyes off me, shook her head, and brushed a hand vaguely across her face, as if to clear away what she had said.

"No, no—oh, Arthur, I'm so sorry for the way I've acted, for blaming you, not believing you, treating you like it's all your fault." She swallowed again and wiped her cheeks with her hands. "I'm so sorry."

"Look, Claire," I said. "Maybe there's a way out of this."

Her head jerked up, and she looked at me.

"We won't bring the police into it—you can go see your father—talk to him, try to convince him to—to—"

I broke off, not knowing what we could say to Tom Cowan. But Claire's face had lit up with eagerness and hope. She wanted so badly to see her father, and I knew that some part of her still believed she could make this turn out all right.

But then her shoulders shook, and she winced. "Oh, Arthur, the pusher—he's after you—he's threatened to kill you." She turned away and grasped the banister. "We have to take those boxes to the police right away, before he—"

I came after her and took her arm. "No, we don't."

She turned to me. "Arthur, I've been risking your life all day with—with my stupid—I'm—"

I could not bear to hear her apologize to me again.

"Listen, Claire, you wanted to know how I came on your car. Why I started this."

"I didn't mean to say that. You don't owe me any explanation—"

"I want to tell you. I was driving around, and I had a gun, and I was trying to build up the nerve to use it on myself."

She gasped, and her hand went to her mouth.

"But I couldn't do it, and then I saw your car, the

kid with the package—" I stopped and took a breath. "You were right. I wanted to get my father. And I hated you, too. That's why I did it; that's why I did everything."

I put out my hand. "Give me the keys to your car, please. I'll take care of it."

She stared at me numbly. "What will you do?"

"I'll take those boxes away and get rid of them. To hell with them. You—you go and settle this thing with your father."

She shook her head. "The pusher thinks you have them. He'll come after you. And when you can't give them to him—"

"He won't find me," I interrupted. I didn't believe that, but I felt no fear any more. "And if I was going to be afraid of him, I should have started two days ago, given him the stuff right away. It's too late now; it's all my responsibility."

But Claire ignored my outstretched hand, turned away, and started down the stairs.

I followed, going on desperately, "You can go to your father, find Angela, set this thing right."

We were on the dark stairs now, and the hollow echo mocked my insistent voice.

Claire paused a moment with her head bowed and turned around. There was not enough light to see her face, but her voice was low and even and authoritative.

"Arthur. This *isn't* your responsibility; it isn't your fault. I can't let you risk your life for what my father has done. We're going to the police."

She stood and waited for me to come down beside her, and we walked down the stairs in silence.

We stepped out into the night. A fresh, biting wind had sprung up and blown the clouds away. Far above us the stars shone faint and chill. Close together we walked across the vast parking lot.

The ordeal wasn't over yet. Soon we would go into

Avon's tidy little police station, the boxes in our hands. We would have to tell the story again and again—to cops, higher-ranking cops, stenographers, district attorneys. And we would end up being brought back here in a squad car to show them Tom Cowan's files, while another car was dispatched to bring him in.

Claire stopped short. Knowing that she could foresee more clearly than I could what was in store for her, I glanced around. Perhaps her courage was faltering. But she was looking straight ahead. I followed her gaze.

We were only a few feet from the Volvo. Its vent window was smashed out.

I ran up and threw open the door—unlocked. The boxes were gone.

She was standing next to me as I straightened up.

"We were stupid to leave them out here."

"But who would know? They look like ordinary cardboard boxes. Who would know what was in them?"

"Tony," I told her. "The pusher. He doesn't know about your father, but he does know Angela's a nurse at Wentworth. He must have put a man out here—"

"And he knows my car, of course," Claire finished despondently. "How stupid—" She broke off, and we stood in silence for a moment.

"Claire," I said at last, "I'm so fucking glad those boxes are gone."

She looked at me, startled. "This doesn't change anything. The proof is in those files. We can still go to the police."

"We don't have to—not now. Tony's got what he wants; he'll leave us alone."

She nodded. We leaned against the car side by side and drew our coats around us.

"Then we have time to go and talk to Dad," she said, her voice dull and haggard. I knew how she felt; at this check to our momentum, my nerves and fatigue had caught up with me. I knew that neither of us could do anything more tonight.

I turned to Claire and said, "I've had it."

She nodded.

"It won't solve anything to put things off."

"No, it won't solve anything."

She sat down sideways in the driver's seat and looked at the keys in her hand. Neither of us wanted to move.

Absurdly, I was reminded of my early dates with Claire. Often, after the movie or concert was over, we had stood beside the car in some dark parking lot, not wanting to give up each other's company.

And now I said what I had often suggested then.

"Claire, would you like to come home and have some tea?"

She looked up at me. "Home?"

"Scarborough Street. My father still owns the place."

Perhaps the memory came back to her, too. Or perhaps it was just the incongruity of it, but she smiled wanly.

There was another still, silent moment, and then she handed me the keys. She moved over to sit with her hands folded in her lap and her head bowed. It was as if the horror of what was to come had kept her going, but with this moment's reprieve, all her energy had gone.

I drove through the lot and stopped at the booth by the exit. As I picked our time slip off the dash, Claire looked up and fumbled in her pockets for change.

"It's all right," I told her. "I'll take care of it."

15

I pulled into our narrow driveway and along the side of the massive, looming house to the back door. Claire got out and stood on the little brick path, and spoke for the first time in half an hour. "Your father never mentioned that he had kept this place."

"I don't know why he does. I guess, what with the property values here, it isn't worth his time to come up and get rid of it."

I stooped and loosened a brick in the path. We always kept a key here, wrapped, for some mysterious reason, in tinfoil. As I found it, Claire spoke.

"I think he keeps it because it was your mother's."

That shook me. I had been living among strangers for so long. And now to be with Claire, who knew me so well . . . I stood and led the way up the creaking wooden steps to the back door.

My feet remembered perfectly the spacing of the stairs inside, and without thought I put out my hand and hit the light switch. The hall was musty and chilly, as if the long winter had gotten into the bones of the old house and it would never be warm again. I turned and went into the kitchen.

I had always had a perverse fondness for our kitchen. It was so unlike the kitchens of new suburban houses, with their built-in electric ranges, recessed refrigerators, quaint little spice racks, and wallpaper with roosters on it. They always looked as if the contractor had jammed in as many efficient gadgets as he could and then laid on a patina of hominess.

Our kitchen had been built in an age that didn't know TV dinners and electric can openers. It was a big, bare room with a worn grey linoleum floor and dingy walls. It had a real pantry, two old and ugly refrigerators (one of which hadn't worked since the early sixties), and in the center of the room a large, square wooden table. I used to sit at that table after school, and my mother would talk to me while she cooked.

There was a squeak of old hinges as Claire opened one of the cabinets. "The cups are here," she said. "Do you really think there's any tea?"

"It would be in the pantry, on the second shelf—"

"I remember," she said and went in.

I told her I would look for a place for us to sit down and slid open the doors that led to the dining room.

In the dark, the long room looked forlorn. The paintings and the crystal chandelier had been taken down, and the long rows of chairs were draped in white cloths. The French windows threw tall rectangles of moonlight on the table, which was uncovered and shone faintly under a white veil of dust.

I stepped through the glass doors into the hall and looked at the front door with its elaborate fanlight. I thought of myself peering in there, then going back to the car to open the packages for the first time, and look with glee at what was inside. Forty-eight hours ago. I turned and went back to the kitchen.

Claire was standing at the table. She had taken off her raincoat; she was wearing a short skirt in a somber plaid, and a rust-colored sweater which was slowly unraveling on the right forearm.

"Found them," she said as she heard my step. She was picking two tea bags out of their little paper envelopes. She was watching what she was doing, and I looked at her, at the broad face with its dark brows and large, clean-lined features, serene and serious but for the wide mouth that always bore traces of her smile.

The teakettle on the stove was rumbling and putting up a plume of steam. I remembered that its top was broken, and it didn't whistle. I picked it up and brought it to the table.

"It's pretty grim in the dining room," I said.

"We always used to sit in here anyway," she answered.

And it was so much like four years ago. She sat at the head of the table, leaning forward, her arms folded along its edge. She did not move except to lift her cup to her lips; and now as then, it never quite seemed to get there because she would pause to say something and forget to drink. I leaned back in the chair beside her, put my feet on the one opposite, and drained my cup at once.

All the immediate, crucial things were too horrible to talk about, so we gratefully let the past take over our minds; every other sentence began, "Do you remember . . ."

"Do you remember the hurdles editorial?"

I looked at her blankly.

"Loomis was planning to buy a new set of hurdles for the spring season—"

I remembered then, and laughed. "Right. I wrote an editorial demanding that the money go to a more worthy cause."

Her brows drew together. "What was the cause?"

"I can't remember, but it was certainly worthy."

She gave me her old sardonic look and went on. "The entire editorial board was here—"

"Eating pizza and re-writing—"

"I don't know that your editorial was getting any better, but it was certainly getting greasier."

"We were on the phone all night—"

"Didn't the headmaster himself call?"

"And half the members of the committee on athletics."

"And that guy—your freaky friend who wouldn't talk much because he thought the narcs were tapping his phone."

We both remembered at the same time that this was Larry Preston. Of course, neither of us said the name, and a dreadful silence fell.

Claire looked down into her teacup and began again. "That track coach—" she said slowly. "He never could figure out what you had against him. Remember, he said you never understood his problems because you were a tennis player?"

That was enough to save us. It led to a comparison of the eccentricities of teachers at Loomis and Chaffee —a subject that was good for nearly an hour.

In the last three years, I had reduced memories of conversations with Claire to transcripts—I remembered only the words and poured over them in isolation to feed my fears and confirm my suspicions. I had forgotten what it was like to be with her, all the things that I had loved about her: the way the light moved in her hair as in a falling stream, lighting up new strands whenever she nodded or shook her head, turning them from brown to gold; the deep-blue eyes that never left me as I spoke, but took in all I said with calm attention; the voice, deep and soft and unhurried, as if there were time for everything.

Suddenly she was saying, "That was really bad— when we met in your father's office the other day. Wasn't it?"

That surprised me. "Bad? You mean bad for me."

"For both of us."

She looked at me.

"I mean, you seemed so cool and aloof. As if we were just acquaintances and we'd seen each other yesterday."

"Oh." She smiled and shook her head. "Arthur, you

know me better than that. You know I put that on
when I'm surprised or ill at ease." Her smile vanished.
"And it was such a shock to see you again—I—"

She broke off and looked at me expectantly, and I
knew she wanted to talk about it. I took my feet off the
chair and leaned forward. This is it, I thought. For
three years I had carried one memory like a stone in
my shoe, plotting the bitter, reproachful things I would
say to her if I got the chance. But now I looked into
that calm, lovely face, and I could not remember any
of them. I said simply, "That time I called you, the day
I left Columbia—"

"Yes," she said at once. Again I was surprised; I
thought she would have forgotten the whole thing by
now.

"I felt you'd let me down, that you didn't care at all."
She nodded. "I know."

"Of course, it was over between us then, but couldn't
you have called back? I was in so much trouble—"

She interrupted. "How was I to know you were in
trouble? I didn't know you were thinking of dropping
out. The first I heard of it was when I got hold of your
roommate a couple of days later, and by that time you
were already gone."

"But I called you that afternoon—"

"Yes, I remember. You wanted to come to Cambridge right away. But there were all sorts of things
I had to do that day; and when I started to tell you,
you got angry and said I was ego-tripping and that
everything I did was a waste of time. Well, I know
you in that mood, and it's no use talking to you. Not
that it was making me feel very good either."

"But I was lonely and in trouble over the strike."

She tossed her hair impatiently. "You didn't say a
thing about any of that to me."

I thought back and realized it was true. I was so
busy attacking her, I'd forgotten why I'd called. True
to form, I attacked now.

"I would have told you if you'd called me back, as you'd promised."

She gave a sigh and looked at me reproachfully. "I did."

My heart turned over. "What?"

"I did call back—again and again. But I got no answer."

"Within an hour?"

She looked at me, bewildered.

"You said you'd call back in an hour."

"Oh." She thought for a moment. "I think I had to go out. I may have been a little late—"

"About five minutes," I said ruefully. The phone had been ringing in my room as I went down in the elevator with my knapsack, ringing all afternoon as I hitched across New Jersey.

She was watching me in complete bafflement now. I explained, "I gave you exactly one hour, then decided you weren't going to call."

Claire shut her eyes. "Oh, Arthur. If things have to be cut that fine . . ." She seemed hurt, even angry, and it surprised me. I still could not believe that she cared.

She opened her eyes and looked at me. "What was I supposed to tell you that was going to turn your life around?"

I was silent. I had never thought of that.

"Why did you have to leave?"

"Because the draft board was after me. If I stuck around, they would have sent me to Indochina to die."

She shook her head. "Your deferment wouldn't have run out until September."

I shrugged helplessly. "You're no fun to argue with, Claire. You've always got all the facts."

But she did not smile back at me. This was all so different from the scene I had imagined during those three lonely years. The roles were reversed—Claire was in the right while I spoke flippantly and evasively.

She sat in silence for a moment, turning her cup nervously in her hands. Then she set it down and looked at me.

"You didn't have to go—you just wanted out. You decided things weren't working very well, and you just let go. Oh, Arthur, you should have stayed. You can make anything work if you care enough."

I looked away. "You always tell me that, Claire. But at that time, things were happening in my life that you didn't know about."

I felt her hand cover mine, and raised my head to find her looking at me with eyes full of sympathy and regret.

"I know. I'm sorry. I've got no right to lecture you. I have no idea what it's like to have your father cut you off—tell you that you can't go to college any more."

I stared at her. "How did you know?"

"He told me when I called him—about a month after it happened."

"You called my father?"

She nodded, took the cup in her hand, and looked at it. "Several times. And your roommates. And your friends. At first people heard from you, but I never got an address. And then for the last year, nothing at all."

Still I stared numbly at her. "Why did you—"

"Because I missed you," she said simply.

"I thought you had forgotten about me."

"Forgotten?"

"I thought we were through as soon as you went to Cambridge."

She frowned, was silent for a moment. "I know. I'm sorry. A lot of new things were happening to me, and I lost track of what was important. Anyway, whenever you called me, you'd tell me I had to march someplace; and when I wasn't crazy about the idea, you'd say something scornful about my selling out." Suddenly she looked up at me and grinned. "Which is not the most satisfactory basis for a relationship, you will admit."

I couldn't help grinning back, and then we both laughed. Her hand still rested in mine, and I squeezed it. It felt so good to be with her again.

"I mean, I don't like to march, and I do want to be a lawyer, but couldn't you forgive me? After all, I did love you. . . ."

She hesitated, and her smile disappeared. She had used the past tense, and it startled and hurt both of us.

"We could have worked it out," she said, "with a little more time, a little more effort."

"Yes . . ." And now it was my turn to hesitate. "We —we still can."

I should not have said it. We had been safe in the past, and now I had brought the future into focus. Claire pulled her hand away from mine and covered her eyes, which had suddenly filled with tears.

"How can we possibly think of that," she said brokenly, "when everything else is so . . ."

I leaned across the table and put my arms around her shuddering shoulders, bringing her head to my chest. "It'll be all right," I said, trying to put conviction into my voice. "There's been no harm done yet. No one else knows."

The dark-gold head nodded, and the voice was once more purposeful. "We'll go see Dad early in the morning. We'll find a way out of this."

"Yes."

She seemed to be all right now, and I straightened up. She let out a long sigh and rose.

"Will you come with me, please?" she asked, with her old proud shyness.

"I'll be with you."

She raised her eyes, and we looked at each other for a long moment. We were too tired to decide anything, too tired to think. We let it happen.

I took a step toward her, and she was in my arms.

* * *

I woke suddenly, and at once looked at my watch. It was 2:30, and we still had hours of the night left, hours when we need do nothing but lie in this dark, quiet room, with the musty sheets around us. I sank back with relief and turned to look at Claire.

She lay on her side, forearms crossed in front of her, the wrists bent and hands tucked beneath her chin. I rolled nearer to her, and she opened her eyes and smiled—I could see the whiteness of her eyes and teeth in the dark. I touched her bent wrist, and she opened her arms, took my hand, and laid it on the warm slope of her breast.

Soon we were both asleep.

16

The shifting of the mattress woke me. Claire was sitting up, her head canted, as if listening. I reached up and touched her smooth, bare back.

She flinched and swung around.

"Someone's in the house!"

And then I heard the steps in the hall outside.

It was that awful, endless moment out of time, when your car goes into a skid on wet pavement, when your feet slide out from under you and you fall backwards into space—when you know something terrible is going to happen, and there is nothing you can do but wait.

The door opened. I saw two dark figures, heard an exclamation, and at once the room burst into light.

Tony stood in the doorway. The flat, light-brown eyes fell on us, and the creases of his cruel grin settled around his mouth. Behind him stood the kid, his hair hanging in dark, greasy bangs over his eyes. He was grinning, too.

"There's nobody else in the house."

Tony waited for confirmation, and I nodded.

"You had an appointment with me, Lavien. But I guess you got distracted."

We were sitting up in the big bed, trying to pull the covers around us. I was shaking violently. I did not wonder why they were here, did not worry about what they were going to do to us. I wanted only to get my clothes on.

They lay in a pile on the floor. Tony stepped over to them, picked up my coat, and began going through the pockets. After a moment I realized what he was looking for.

"I don't have the gun any more."

He ignored me, picked up the trousers, and patted the pockets. Then he dropped them and straightened up.

"Get dressed."

I leaped out of bed, grabbed my pants, and pulled them on. Tony had walked away; he was peering into the empty shelves. But the kid at the door kept his eyes on us. In the bed Claire hesitated, reluctant to give up the protection of the covers. I stepped between her and the kid, grabbed her clothes, and tossed them to her.

The kid watched all this with a thin smile. Then I saw what he held in his right hand.

He had a gun, now pointed carelessly at the floor. It wasn't a little .32 like the one I had threatened Tony with. It was a .44 magnum revolver. I knew enough about guns to recognize it, and now I was really scared. It is illegal to carry a .44 because people who get hit with one die. If they are hit in the head or the chest, they die immediately. If not, they die slowly of shock and loss of blood. It is not a gun for impressing people. It is for killing.

I turned to Tony. He was bending low to look under a chair in the corner of the room.

"What do you want of us?" My voice was a choked whisper.

"Where is it?" he said without turning.

I was literally scared out of my wits. I could not understand what he meant.

When I didn't answer, he straightened up slowly and turned. He was pale, and his mouth was set. I had seen that look of fatigue and desperation a lot tonight, and I realized that he was just as frightened as the rest of us.

"Don't be stupid, kid," he said, and his voice was earnest, not his usual bullying tone. "Give me the packages right now."

At last I understood. "I don't have them. Somebody stole them from the car about nine tonight."

He stared at me uncomprehendingly.

"I've got a schedule to keep, kid. I can't let you cost me twenty thousand dollars!"

There was pure hatred in his voice, and unconsciously I stepped back. I knew he was keying himself up to beat my face in, if he had to.

"Look," I said. "We left the stuff in the car, and somebody broke the window and took it."

The wrinkles gathered on his low forehead; he seemed to hear what I was saying for the first time.

"The car in the driveway?"

"Yes."

He walked over to the kid at the door. "Check it out, Scott," he said. He held out his hand for the gun and the kid gave it to him, then turned and went out the door. We could hear his footsteps on the stairs.

Tony leaned against the jamb and folded his arms, watching us through half-closed eyes. He was wearing flared double-knit slacks in a bright check; a khaki safari jacket, neatly buttoned and belted; and a gold shirt, open at the neck. The collar was fashionably large and folded outside his coat so that the points reached nearly to his armpits. He looked like a junior sales manager at the company barbecue, and I remembered that before I had thought his studied modishness funny. Now it frightened me; there was something inhuman about it.

I looked at the heavy blue-black gun and hoped desperately that when Scott came back and reported that the window was really smashed, they would leave us alone.

Again the hurried steps on the staircase, and Scott appeared at the door. Tony looked at him, and he nodded.

Once more the flat tan eyes were on me. Consciously I lowered my gaze to his mouth. Whatever emotion he felt seemed never to reach his eyes.

He watched me for a long moment, then addressed Scott without turning. "Take the girl downstairs. Don't turn on any more lights."

Claire and I looked at each other. There was nothing I could do, and I thought it was better this way. Tony did not know the Volvo belonged to Claire, did not know who she was. She would be safer away from him.

She seemed to understand and crossed the room. As she passed Tony, he put his hand on her arm, still not taking his eyes off me.

"Don't make any noise, and you'll be O.K. Understand?"

She gave me a last worried glance and went out with Scott. Tony shut the door, put his back to it, and folded his arms again.

"Now, Lavien, even if I believe you, this doesn't solve my problem. I'm still out some very expensive merchandise, and it's your fault. Ergo, you got to make up the loss. See what I mean?"

"But what can I do? It was stolen."

He gave a tired, humorless smile and straightened up. His hands fell to his sides. I stared at the gun.

"That Volvo," he said, "that's the car Scott was supposed to make the pickup from. And it turns out to be yours. Now there are certain aspects of this operation I've never liked, and right now somebody's trying to put one over on me."

He advanced a step toward me. "The source is somebody at Wentworth Hospital, somebody who's helping Angela. You know who it is. And you're gonna tell me."

I stalled for time. "Look, I know about Angela, but that's all."

Again he seemed not to hear me and advanced another step. His face was only a foot from mine.

"You're lying, Lavien. I don't know who you are or what you've got to do with this, but I'm getting tired of you. Tell me who the source is, now."

And then, suddenly, I wasn't afraid any more. Claire had suffered a great deal to keep her father safe from the police, and I knew I would not betray her to a cheap tough guy who dressed like a fag white hunter.

"I'm tired of you, too, asshole," I said steadily.

There was no change in his expression, no warning at all.

He hit me with a quick, short, almost negligent sweep of his right arm. There was no weight behind the blow, but with the gun in his hand, there didn't have to be. It seemed to jar my skull off my spine.

There was another shock as my knees hit the floor. My cheek burned; the blade sight had ripped the skin open. I saw the little drops of blood falling onto my pants.

He put a hand under my jaw and pulled me up. I looked dully into the set, expressionless face and didn't see the gun butt swing down and into my stomach.

I toppled over, gasping, trying to pull some air into my lungs. After an eternity breath returned, pushing the pain down out of my chest. I lay flat and pulled my arms in, turning my face into the carpet. I waited for the blow to fall on my back.

But it didn't come. Then I realized that Tony was talking. I wanted to answer—to do anything that would postpone the next wave of pain. But I couldn't understand what the voice was saying.

Suddenly a hand touched my neck. I winced and tried to turn away. I wouldn't let him get at my face.

Again I heard a voice, a different voice. Soft, at my ear. It was Claire's.

"Arthur, it's O.K. now," she was saying.

I turned a little and buried my face in the rough wool of her skirt, and felt her arms cover my shoulders. I was safe.

Now I could understand Tony's voice.

"How do we know this is true?"

"Look in the phone book," she answered tiredly. "You'll see his office number at Wentworth."

"Cowan?"

"C–o–w–a–n. Thomas."

I got my hands under me and straightened up. Claire was kneeling beside me. She took the edge of a sheet and dabbed the blood off my cheek.

"Thanks, Arthur," she whispered. "But it wasn't worth it."

I nodded and looked up at Tony.

He was leaning against the doorjamb, arms folded and eyes half shut, as if the last few minutes hadn't happened. But there was one difference—his hands were empty. The gun had disappeared. He was waiting patiently; presently his square jaw descended as if on hinges, and he yawned silently. I looked at my watch: four thirty.

Scott came in with a telephone directory open in his hands. He showed it to Tony, pointing at a name. Tony hardly glanced at it. He turned, not to me, but to Claire. He seemed to have forgotten about me.

"Your old man will be at home now?"

She nodded.

"How many people in the house?"

At that she hesitated.

"Take it easy," he said at once. "For a man in my position it would be counter-productive to shake up my source of supply. There'll be no trouble."

She glanced at me, and I nodded. I believed Tony. I didn't think he would harm Tom.

"He's alone."

Tony nodded. "O.K. Let's go."

Of course, we had not expected that he would leave us behind. We didn't even want that. Now we would see this thing through to the end.

Claire helped me up, but I found that I was quite steady on my feet. He had hit me low on the jawbone, a blow that hurt but did little damage. He was good at his work.

Tony led the way, and the kid, Scott, fell in behind me. I looked at his hands, and they were empty, too. Tony was not worried that we would try to run now.

Claire pressed her damp palm against mine, and we went down the wide front staircase and crossed the great, highceilinged hall. Tony swung open the front door and said over his shoulder, "You can open locks like this with a credit card. Won't do for a fancy place like this."

He had his loud, cheerfully bullying tone again; the fear and violence of a few minutes ago were forgotten. I realized that he must be delighted to find out, at last, Tom Cowan's name. A great deal of trouble had been taken to keep the information from him.

As we stepped out on the porch, I suddenly had a vivid image of the two men sliding the lock open, moving carefully, quietly, through the big house, checking all the rooms. What Claire must have felt when she woke to hear those small sounds and realized they were footsteps. I squeezed her hand and drew her closer to me.

"Tony," I said, "how did you find us?"

I half expected him to turn and tell me to shut up or he'd hit me again, but he seemed glad to talk.

"Scott and Joe called me up, said they nearly had you when you got grabbed by the cops. They figured the deal was up and wanted to go home, but I told 'em to stick around. I figured you'd be back, that the cops only busted you on account of you're so crummy-looking, and they'd let you go when they found out you were a rich kid. I was right, huh?"

"Yeah," I said. I could see no point in telling him the whole story. He went on.

"Well, a couple of hours later you came along in the Volvo. Scott was waiting on Forty-second in a car, and he tailed you up here. But he doesn't know a god-damn thing about Hartford, and he lost you as soon as it got dark."

Before we reached Jim's.

"Then how did you find us?"

He looked over his shoulder, and his lips drew back from his teeth. He was grinning. "I had to come up here myself and do something this clown hadn't thought of. I looked in the phone book under Lavien, Arthur."

He seemed to invite me to join him in his amuse-ment at the kid's stupidity, so I did.

"That's a weird name, Lavien. Jewish?"

"No."

"You act Jewish, Lavien," he observed. "You're a pain in the ass."

Tony had prudently left his car on the street and ap-proached the house on foot. It was a big, expensive car, twenty feet of extravagantly curved metal, its blue surface reflecting the street lamps in sinuous bends of light. It had red pinstripes, a monogram on the door, and a vinyl roof with opera windows that looked as tiny and inadequate as the eyes of a whale.

Tony opened the door and gestured. Claire and I got in the back and sank deep into the velour uphol-stery. The interior lights stayed on as Tony and Scott got in the front seats, and I could see our faces in the mirror. We were pale but we no longer looked frightened.

And I *was not* frightened of Tony any more. He had hit me, not out of sadism or hatred but out of a sense of wounded self-esteem. He was now himself again, not a tough guy but a conceited, aggressive small businessman, with a loud voice, fancy clothes, and a big car. He was dangerous only when things were going badly for him. Right now he thought he would get his "shipment," and he was expansive. I meant to take advantage of that, to find out what I could from him.

Scott started the engine, and silently, smoothly, we pulled away. It was a strange ride. We made our way through the dark and quiet streets of West Hartford, Claire giving toneless directions to Scott while I fed questions to Tony, who offered loud, lengthy replies.

"You've got quite a business going, Tony," I began.

He was leaning back comfortably against the headrest, and I could see only his small ear, his neatly trimmed sideburn, and the tip of his short nose.

"Yeah," he said. "I do pretty well."

"I know pills are pretty lucrative, but do you do well in morphine?"

He answered at once. He did not consider whether he should tell me these things; he just liked to talk.

"I don't deal in morphine. Hard stuff's not the territory for an independent like me. You deal morphine, shit like that, you got the cops after you, you got an unstable clientele, and worst of all you got the Mob, the big guys. Then there's the problem of supply. Only niggers who don't want to live long get into pushing hard stuff." Again he told me the story of the black guy who ended up in the Harlem River.

At last he finished. "No, I got a solid operation, and I don't mess around. Downers, they're the real growth market. People—affluent people—are gonna need 'em more and more, what with the stresses of modern life and all."

I considered this sociological insight as Claire gave a direction to Scott, then asked, "But what about the stuff you give Angela?"

"Oh, that. That's strictly small quantities. And it's a means to an end. Like I say, it's the pills I'm after. Of course, there's a marginal risk, but you gotta take chances in business. And it's worth it to keep a hold on that chick."

There was another pause as Claire said, "Left here," and then Tony resumed, enjoying the talk.

"It's the best of both worlds I got. If your source is an addict, she's reliable, she needs you even more 'n you need her. But downers, uppers, they're a milder habit, and that's good. You get a stable market, a better class of clientele. People I supply are well off, most of 'em. Nice homes, plenty of money. And all kinds of people take uppers—college kids, truck drivers—you'd be surprised."

He had run down for a moment, so I fed him another line.

"You were pretty smart to get hold of Angela."

"Man, you aren't kiddin'," he said vehemently. "When this—uh, when one of my sources let me know there was a junkie nurse lookin' for a connection, I knew it was my lucky day."

I thought of saying that I knew Larry but resisted the temptation. I didn't want to shake Tony.

He turned in his seat, warming to the subject. "See, there's a lot of people in the medical profession who have a habit—more than twice the incidence in the general population, and that's a fact."

I nodded appreciatively, and he settled back.

"Turn right at these lights," said Claire softly.

The lights went red and the kid stopped.

"Jump 'em, dummy. There's nobody around." He glanced around and grinned at me, again inviting me to join him in ridiculing Scott. Tony liked to have allies.

Then he put his head back against the headrest and continued. "Now, when one of these people comes outside looking for a connection, you're set if you can get hold of 'em. See, the problem in pills is supply. Distribution any jerk can handle."

Claire gave another direction.

"I played it very cool with this girl. Had to. She was real nervous about dealin' with me, really scared. So we started out on a cash basis. And eventually, sure enough, she came to me and said she couldn't pay any more, but she had to have the stuff."

He chuckled pleasurably. "So I suggested she pay with downers. I acted like it was strictly a favor to her, but that was what I was after all along, of course. She didn't like the idea. She was a real cunt about it, as a matter of fact. But there was nothing else she could do, and she went along with me in the end."

I thought of Angela, and I shuddered. To fall into the hands of somebody like Tony . . .

"Straight," Claire said. Tony was silent for a while; and when he spoke again, the pleasure had drained out of his voice.

"But addicts have this one big problem—they're unreliable." He meant one problem as far as he was concerned, of course. "Angela's been a real mess lately. And then there was that fuckup Wednesday."

Suddenly he seemed to remember to whom he was talking, and he swiveled around to look from one of us to the other.

"So, it's your old man who's the source," he said to Claire. She didn't respond, but he nodded and went on. "That was another thing about Angela. I knew someone was helping her, but she'd never let on who it was. And since Wednesday I haven't been able to find her at all."

He looked troubled, but after a moment he shrugged and turned back in his seat.

"Well, I found out anyway."

There was silence for a moment. Claire's voice trembled as she gave a direction, and I saw that we were turning onto her street.

Abruptly Tony turned around again and looked at her.

"Say, is that Volvo yours?"

"Yes," said Claire tiredly. "But I didn't know anything about what my father was doing."

He took that in, then turned to me.

"Until your boyfriend here came along. How did you find out about it?"

I shrugged. "Coincidence. I just saw the car."

I didn't expect him to believe me, but he nodded slowly.

"Lavien, you have screwed things up royally."

It was my turn to nod.

"Stop," said Claire. "This is it."

17

Tony got out and waited, preferring for us to lead the way up the hill to the house. I noticed that there were lights on in the hall and one of the bedrooms. Whether Jim had called him or not, I doubted that Tom Cowan had slept at all tonight.

We crossed the lawn, casting long black shadows in the moonlight. Beneath the grass, the soggy ground squelched under our feet.

We were ten feet from the front porch when the lights went on and the door opened. Tom stepped out. Claire and I stopped, and for a moment no one spoke.

The sight of him shook me. He was pale and tired, like the rest of us, but it was more than that. He had a look I had seen only once before—on my mother's face, during the last months of her illness, when she was beyond fear and only wanted the suffering to end.

Tony stepped up beside me.

"Glad to meet you, Dr. Cowan."

His tone was hearty, as if he wanted to reach out and shake Tom's hand. The cruelty of it almost made me gasp, and then I looked at Tony and realized that he was not trying to be cruel. He really was glad to meet Tom and incapable of understanding that Tom might feel differently about it.

Tom's eyes were on Claire; but as Tony spoke, he jerked his head around with a visible effort to face him. This man had dominated Tom's thoughts for so long, and Tom had wished so fervently that he would never have to see him.

Tony continued. "If we can just step inside for a moment, we'll settle this matter, and you can go back to sleep."

That was almost laughable; Tom had obviously not been to bed. He wore yesterday's clothes—grey flannels and a beautiful shirt in pinstripes of light and dark blue. Tom always wore fine shirts.

Wordlessly he stepped back to let us enter. As Claire passed him, he put a hand on her arm and said quietly, "Claire, take one of the cars and get away from here. Take Arthur with you."

She answered tonelessly, without raising her head, "Dad, I know about—about the whole thing."

He stood looking at the crown of her head, and his dark eyes narrowed with pain as he wondered what his daughter must think of him.

Tony stood surveying the hall. He looked at everything as if he were considering buying it and meant to make a smart deal. Eventually he turned to Tom.

"Let's go and sit down, Dr. Cowan, and get this thing ironed out."

Tom turned and pushed a sliding door open. We went into the study, a small room that Mrs. Cowan had furnished richly in blues and browns. There were big easy chairs and tall bookcases, now in darkness because only the desk lamp was on, throwing light over the small glass-topped desk, which was always covered by a blanket of medical journals.

Tom went behind it and sat down heavily, resting his elbows high on the arms of the chair so that his shoulders hunched up as if to ward off blows. There was only one chair before the desk, and Tony took it. He sat back comfortably, stretched his right leg out and dug the heel into the carpet, then crossed the other leg over. He looked as if he had designed this pose to communicate relaxed authority. Claire and I stopped by the edge of the desk; neither of us felt like sitting down. I glanced over my shoulder. The kid, Scott, had stationed himself at the sliding door.

I turned back to find Tom staring at me. It was a look without emotion, without reproach, without curiosity. It said simply, "You have done this."

I stared coldly back at him, remembering that he had done his best to frame me and put me in prison. It must have shown in my eyes, for he nodded sadly and looked away.

"O.K.," Tony began. "I'm sure you know what's happening here. Your daughter's boyfriend got hold of our shipment, and now he's lost it." He swung his head in my direction and grinned sourly, inviting Tom to join in his disgust for me, just as he had earlier invited me to laugh at Scott.

Tom turned to me. "Lost it?"

I nodded. "It was stolen from Claire's car outside Wentworth a few hours ago."

He looked down at his hands, folded them. "There are always thieves watchin' the lots. They know there are likely to be drugs in some of the cars." The soft, drawling voice was expressionless. Suddenly he looked up at Claire.

"What were you doing at Wentworth?"

She looked away.

"Well, immaterial of that," Tony went on loudly, "my problem at this point in time is simple. In my line of work, your customers won't wait on you. So, Dr. Cowan, you'll have to go out to the hospital tonight and get me a replacement for my shipment, in full."

Tom shook his head. "I can't do that."

Tony uncrossed his legs and leaned forward. "What do you mean, you can't?"

"It takes a full month to get a"—he grasped at Tony's euphemism—"shipment together. I can't do anything for you tonight."

He raised his eyes to meet Tony's. His gaze was like Claire's, level and direct. I knew that to Tony it would appear stubborn.

"But you're a doctor! You can get drugs if you need them, and don't tell me different!"

Tony's cheerful, overbearing confidence had gone as quickly as it had come. He was standing now, as if carried out of the chair by the momentum of his anger. His legs were bent and braced, and his arms curled slightly forward. Again he looked like the man who had beaten me, and again I was afraid. I looked at the side pocket of his coat and saw the square bulge of the gun.

Tom's gaze did not waver. "I have maybe five Amytal capsules in my office. That's all."

Tony glared back at him. "You can get more!"

Deliberately, exhaustively, Tom began to explain the FDA regulations, the method he used to get around them, and the impossibility of collecting a large supply of drugs quickly.

All the time, Tony maintained his tensed, crouched stance, like a man trying to keep his feet on a rolling deck. Beads of sweat crawled slowly from his thick, wiry hair and ran down his forehead. When Tom ceased his explanation, Tony began, loudly and incoherently, to tell him about distribution schedules, networks of contacts, and the impatient clients who would go elsewhere if he let them down.

When he finished, Tom again began to explain the FDA rules.

It was frightening; it would almost have been funny. As they went on, I began to understand that Tony and Tom were bound together by more than this drug connection; they were both so blindly selfish that each believed that anything he needed badly enough would be given to him. Neither of them would give in. They were simply talking each other into desperation, and I knew which one would crack first.

"No, I can't go to the pharmacy and demand a quantity of pills because—" Tom began for the second time. But Tony interrupted.

He lunged at the desk, tore his eyes away from Tom to scan it, and snatched up a glass paperweight. He lifted it high above his head and dashed it to the floor. It hit the thick carpet with a thud and began to roll, unbroken. Tony pursued it and kicked it against a wall. Still it would not shatter. He jerked his head up and pointed a thick, gold-ringed finger at Tom.

"I'm gonna search this house!"

Tom looked at him, bewildered. "You won't find anything. I don't keep supplies of drugs here."

Tony backed up a step, his hand still outstretched. "You better hope I find something, or . . ."

His head swiveled and he looked at Claire. His mouth worked, searching for a threat. I began to shiver. This is how murder happens, I thought. It isn't planned. Somebody gets angry, desperate, and there is a gun within reach. It had done Tony no good to kick the paperweight, and it would do him no good to harm Claire. But he needed to destroy something of Tom's, and only the sanctions of the law would make her life matter to him more than a piece of crystal. And he might be past remembering them.

Abruptly he spun around and lurched across the room. He stopped at the door and jerked the gun out of his pocket.

I was paralyzed with fear. If he had pointed the gun at Claire, I could not have reached him or thrown myself in front of her. I could not have moved.

But he only jammed it in Scott's hands.

"They stay where they are till I get back!" he shouted and went out the door. A few remaining shreds of logic drove him to the bathroom, where he was more successful at breaking things.

I looked at Tom. He was standing now, staring at

the gun in Scott's hand. At last something had broken through his fatigue and despair.

He turned on me. "How could you bring these men into my home, Arthur? How could you put Claire in such danger?"

I was too shaken to protest. And he was right, after all. I had started it.

Claire raised her head and spoke in a hushed voice. "It was you, Dad. You got me involved when you decided to use Jim—"

She spoke without reproach; almost gently. But Tom interrupted quickly, as if he could not bear to hear a word more.

"No—no. It was the girl who forced me to . . ."

And then it hit me. It was so obvious, but we had all been too frightened to think it out.

"Tom," I said, "has Angela called you?"

He looked at me blankly. "Called me—when?"

"Tonight."

He shook his head vehemently, as if this proved his innocence. "No. I haven't heard from her since Wednesday. I don't know where she is. She—"

He broke off; we all heard Tony's swift, heavy footsteps on the stairs.

He strode into the room, jerking the gun out of Scott's hands. I turned and stepped up to him.

"Angela's got the stuff."

The hard tan eyes settled on me, and at once the creases of tension and meanness around his mouth began to ease. He wanted to believe me.

"Angela?"

"She was desperate by this evening. Say she came back to Wentworth to try to steal a couple of ampules of morphine. Say she spotted the Volvo—she knows it was used for the drop in the first place. And when she looked inside it, she saw the boxes."

He nodded eagerly, and then his brows drew together worriedly. "But how the hell do we find her?"

"She'll call Dr. Cowan to let him know what happened. Maybe this morning."

His eyes went to Tom, flicked back to me. "How do you know?"

"Because she's going to run through what she's got pretty soon, and then she'll need more. Without you or Dr. Cowan, how's she going to get it?"

He thought it over for a moment, and then he straightened up and rocked his weight back on his heels. He had regained his equilibrium as quickly as a squalling baby once it gets its bottle.

He grinned past me at Tom. "Sure. I was dumb not to think of that before. And there's another reason, ain't there, Doc?"

Tom watched him silently. I knew what was coming next.

"She's your girlfriend, right, Doc?"

He sank back in his chair and said in a tired, disgusted voice. "Is that what she tells you?"

"Oh, no. Angela never mentioned your name. But it kinda fits, doesn't it? I mean, why else would you do all this for her?"

Tom said harshly, "She's not my girlfriend." As he spoke, he glanced quickly at Claire.

So did I. Her head was bowed, and I could see that her eyes were closed.

Tony shrugged equably: he wasn't really very interested. "O.K. Whatever you say."

And then for ten minutes there was a grim silence. My legs were throbbing, but not for anything could I have moved across the room to a chair. Claire stood motionless beside me, her head down. But when I touched her hand with mine, she took it and squeezed it tightly. Tom watched her steadily, and he too was immobile but for the slight, continuous working of his jaw muscles that sent ripples across his stubbled cheek. Only Tony was restless; his foot tapped continually, his crossed legs swayed, and his eyes wandered about the room. He noticed that the heavy revolver was still in his hand, and with a grin he shoved it back in his pocket.

From time to time all of us except Claire glanced at the phone on the desk. It was an elaborate phone, with several lines and a speaker attachment. But it remained mute.

Finally, mercifully, Tony stood up and stretched.

"I'm going to help myself to some coffee, Doc," he announced and strolled to the door. On his way out he casually pulled the gun from his pocket and tossed it to Scott, as if it were a set of car keys. Scott fumbled the catch, and the gun fell. He swiftly bent to pick it up.

"Nice goin', kid. You nearly shot your leg off." Tony grinned at us and left the room.

Very deliberately Claire raised her head and looked into her father's eyes. He spoke first.

"I'm sorry I told Jim to use your car, Claire. If only I hadn't. . . ."

She winced at the inadequacy of that, but he went on, as if confessing to this one fault would excuse him. Or perhaps it was the only thing he really felt sorry for. He seemed to feel no responsibility for Jim or Angela or me. Claire and her mother took up all the attention he was capable of devoting to people.

"I took no part in the deliveries. I knew nothin' about this man until two days ago."

His drawling voice had grown so soft I could hardly hear it. Claire let go of my hand and started to move around the desk.

Tom followed her with his eyes. "Then, early in the evening, Angela called me, told me she couldn't leave the hospital, and the delivery had to go that night. She wanted *me* to do it." He said that as if it were a brutally unjust demand. "Well, I told her I couldn't leave the hospital either. There was a staff meeting. . . ." He began, earnestly and exhaustively, to explain to us the importance of the staff meeting.

But we knew that had nothing to do with it. It was the act of actually, physically, handing drugs over to a pusher that Tom could not face.

Instead he thought of Jim—Jim who was near at hand, who would be willing to do a favor for his girl-friend's father. Very carefully, very quickly, in his office on that Wednesday evening, he had worked out the errands to the two doctors, one real and one false, and the two identical boxes. But for me, Jim would never have known what he had done.

Claire reached back to pull up a chair and sat down at her father's side. He looked at her a little fearfully now; he knew what she would ask next.

"Dad, why did you begin—supplying this girl in the first place?"

He said listlessly, "She was pilfering ampules of morphine from the hospital. She had to be stopped or there would have been a scandal."

Claire cut in softly, "Dad, is she"—she hesitated, and Tom closed his eyes, like a driver who realizes he cannot avoid a wreck—"is she your lover?"

There was a pause, and then he said slowly, "No. It was a mistake."

At first I thought he was referring to what Tony had said. But he meant something else.

"I had a party for the surgery staff here on New Year's Eve. I had to give it; it was my turn. We all enjoyed ourselves. Perhaps we had a little too much to drink."

He stopped then and looked reflectively into a dark corner of the room. I remembered that his wife had always tried to convince him that he was an alcoholic.

"She—Angela—stayed after everyone was gone to help me clean up. Jean was away in Boston. We—" he broke off, took a breath. "It was only once. Afterwards I tried to stay away from her as much as possible." He shook his head. "I don't think anyone ever knew. I'm sure . . ."

I suppose it was inevitable that Tom would have an affair and that it would be like this. He did not want love but guilt. He owed so much to his wife, yet he had ceased to love her; and in some strange way, it was easier for him if he was bound to her by some sin. He had lived his private life for the last ten years as if suffering in atonement; now at last he had something to be guilty of. It must almost have been a relief.

He told us the whole story then, in brief disconnected sentences, broken by long, dead silences, as if he could see the whole thing before him but could manage to drag out and say aloud only the bare facts.

He had known nothing about Angela's habit—he had barely spoken to her, after all. He had not been alarmed when the punctilious Van Brocken came and told him that the figures from one of the surgery wards did not tally with the pharmacy's. He had said it must be a paperwork error, and would Tom please tell his nurses to be sure and write up every ampule they used?

Tom had suspected nothing, but hospitals are very discreet about such things, and he had set up private appointments with each of the sixteen nurses who worked on the fifth floor. He had been shaken to see Angela's name among them and dreaded a private meeting with her.

It was to be far, far worse than he had imagined. No doubt he was elaborately kind to her, either out of guilt or because her loveliness touched him. Angela was lonely and scared, and when he mentioned the morphine shortage, she broke down and confessed everything to him.

It devastated Tom. That he had committed adultery was bad enough, but that the girl should turn out to be a junkie . . . He felt that she was dirty, that she had defiled him.

More than that, he feared that she would cause a

scandal at Wentworth. Perhaps he even felt that his own sin would come out. He lost his temper and told her that she must not take another ampule.

She had started to cry then. She wanted to do what he said, but she had to have morphine, and she knew no other way to get it.

I could see him storming at her, threatening her, as he paced over the thick blue carpet of his quiet, luxurious office, while she wept miserably in her chair. But finally, in the face of her need and his own guilt, he had given in. He began to supply her with morphine from the office, covering up by writing false prescriptions, as he was later to do with the pills.

This had gone on for a month, a month of continual fear and self-disgust for Tom.

I looked at Claire and knew that she was thinking how alone he had been with his misery. His wife spoke to him only when her bitterness boiled over, and his brilliant, beloved daughter was far away and caught up in her own busy life.

Finally, just as Tom's nerves could bear it no longer, he remembered Larry Preston. Larry was well known among the parents of Loomis and Chaffee kids, and Tom had heard somewhere that he was heavily involved in the New York drug scene. He found out Larry's address and gave it to Angela, and told her that he would do no more for her, that she was on her own.

For a few weeks then he hardly saw her. He threw himself into his busy routine of surgery and administration, and ceased to think about her.

It had been a cruel shock to him to come out of the O.R. one day and see her waiting for him. At once he had feared the worst: that her connection had broken down.

"If she had started to steal morphine again . . ." He said no more, but we understood. Then, surely, there would have been an investigation. And the fact that he had supplied her would have come out. Now he was guilty, too.

So he was almost relieved when Angela told him the pusher knew she was a nurse and had demanded barbiturates as payment. For the last few months, Tom had carefully hoarded pills and given them to her. After that he never knew what became of them. It was almost easy for him; there was little risk, and the guilt he had felt for giving morphine to a woman he had slept with was less now that he was only supplying soft drugs to people he never saw.

The whole time he talked, Claire never took her eyes off him. Her gaze was full of pain and kindness, unjudging, and it would have helped Tom had he looked at her. But he never did; he stared fixedly into the darkness.

She leaned close to him now, and her voice was even softer than his.

"Oh, Dad, why didn't you persuade her to get help when she first told you she was an addict?"

"There would have been a scandal. She'd have been fired, imprisoned. . . ."

"They don't treat people like that now. She could have gotten help—" She broke off. Her hands rose to cover her face, but with an effort she stopped them.

"Why couldn't you have tried to pull her out of this instead of sinking into it yourself?" It was almost a wail; she could not control her voice now to whisper.

Still Tom did not look at her. His jaw muscles tightened, and he spoke so quickly and quietly that we could hardly hear him.

"The moment I—went to bed with her, I knew I'd become as bad as she is."

He would say no more, and for a full minute there was silence.

Then the phone rang.

Tom jumped and stared at it but made no move to answer. Then as it rang a second time he snatched the receiver up, fending off the sound as if it were a blow.

For a moment then I hoped that I had been wrong, hoped it was not Angela. I had not thought of her at all; I had only wanted something to throw between Claire and Tony. I had remembered her weakness when the others had forgotten, and I had used her. But the expression on Tom's face as he listened told me I had been right.

"No, you're not disturbing me. What do you want?"

Tony came in quickly, with a half-eaten sandwich in his hand. He walked to the desk and pressed the switch on the speaker. At once we could hear Angela's voice.

". . . was about to go in, try to get something from the nurses' station." She sounded breathless and excited but also relieved. "I'm—I'm sorry, Tom. I knew I shouldn't do it, but I was in really bad shape."

"If you were in bad shape, that's all the more reason you shouldn't have gone into Wentworth," said Tom harshly. I winced for Angela. He just didn't understand at all.

"I know—I'm real sorry. I could have gotten us both in trouble. But the pain was like really bad. I—I could hardly move—and I kept driving around and around the parking lot, and then I saw the car." She told him about the packages inside and her delight at seeing them.

"That was your daughter's car, wasn't it?" she asked.

"Yes."

Angela spoke with concern. "Have you seen her tonight? Is she all right?"

He hesitated a moment, then said yes.

"Was there—was there a guy with her, a guy named Arthur?"

Again Tom gave a guarded yes. He seemed to fear that she was trying to get something out of him.

"Listen," she said urgently, "this guy Arthur—the pusher's after him; he's threatened to kill him."

I felt ashamed. She was trying to help me, which was more than I had ever done for her.

Again Tom paused a moment.

"The pusher?" he said blankly.

"Yes—Tony, the guy I'm getting the shit from. You haven't heard from him?"

Tom looked up at Tony, who shook his head.

"No."

"Well, listen. I've got the pills, too, and I think we should let him have them. 'Cause if he finds Arthur or if he finds out who you are . . ."

Tom leaned forward. "You want to arrange a meeting with this fellah Tony?"

"No, not me." We could hear her take a broken breath and go on. "Listen. I'm sorry, but I can't get near him again. That night—it wasn't my fault when the shipment got lost, and he had plenty more morphine, but he wouldn't give me a single lousy shot until he got his fucking pills. He's mean—he's a bad man."

I looked at Tony. He put down his sandwich and brushed off his fingers.

"I'm sorry, Tom. But you'll have to get the pills from me and—and arrange it. I won't deal with Tony any more."

"Angela, listen, you'll have to deal with him. You'll run out of stuff in a couple of weeks—"

"No, we—we'll have to go back to the way we were doing it before. You'll have to get the stuff for me." Her voice was tired and sorry but determined. "I wish—oh, I don't know, but we just can't deal with Tony. We just can't."

Tom raised his head and met Tony's eyes. For a long moment they looked at each other.

Then Tony leaned forward and flipped off the speaker. He straightened up and gestured to Tom.

Angela said something, and he replied, "Yes, just a minute." He put down the receiver and followed Tony to the door.

Tony whispered an order to the kid and gave him the gun. Then he and Tom went out and slid the door closed behind them. The kid walked around the desk and picked up the receiver. He listened a moment, waiting for Tom to pick up the extension in the hall, and hung up. The gun barrel was pointed exactly between Claire and me.

Neither of us moved, and for several minutes nothing happened.

Finally the doors slid open and the two men returned. The change in them was extraordinary. Tom returned to his chair and settled into it heavily with a sigh—a sigh of relief. Although he still seemed very tired, there was a clear, unworried look to his face. But a swift, tight quality had come into Tony's movements, and his hard face was set and almost white. When he reached out to take the revolver from Scott, I noticed that the sweat had soaked through his khaki jacket under the arms and across the shoulders.

"Where are the keys?" He spoke softly now, and there was something alarming about that.

"They're on hooks by the back door."

He turned to Scott. "Take one of Cowan's cars. Leave it at the station and go back to the city. I'll call you later."

Scott looked confused, but wordlessly turned to the door. Tony's eyes fell on us, and he called to him, "Wait. Take them with you. Drive out west aways, and leave 'em where they can't cause any trouble for a while. Don't hurt 'em."

The last sentence was added for Tom's benefit, but he stood and said angrily, "No! My daughter stays here."

Tony thought about this. "All right—take him though."

Claire stood and swiftly crossed the room to take my hand. Tony's flat eyes turned on me.

"You won't get hurt, Lavion. And it'll be a lot better all around if you go."

I believed him, and I was so glad he was leaving that I would have cooperated. I was as weak as Cowan.

But Claire held onto my hand. "If Arthur goes, so do I."

"Oh, for Christ's sake!" Tony exploded with frustration. He spun and faced Tom.

"O.K. They stay. But I mean, they *stay*. Understand?"

Cowan nodded.

Still Tony looked at him. "You're sure you can handle it?"

"Yes," Tom answered.

Tony turned and followed Scott to the door. There he paused and addressed all of us.

"You'll never have to see me again. If you're smart, you'll treat this whole thing like a bad car accident and forget it."

Then he was gone. After a moment, we heard the cars pulling away.

Claire spun around and leaned across the desk. Her father did not look up at her.

"What did you do out there?"

He made a vague gesture with his right hand. "I've convinced Angela to meet him, to give him the pills. And that will be the end of it."

I stared at him and realized that he did not know he was lying to us. He really had blocked out what had happened in the hall. I would have believed him if I had not heard Angela's frightened voice as she said she would never deal with Tony again, had not seen Tony's face as he took the gun.

Claire and I knew then. We had seen it in the look Tom and Tony exchanged: Angela is dangerous to us. Their eyes had agreed upon it.

"Oh, God," Claire whispered in horror. "Oh, God."

I lunged over the desk. "She's expecting to meet you, isn't she?"

He raised his dark, mournful eyes to mine.

"Tom, you've got to tell us where."

He sighed and looked away. "No, Arthur."

I tried to pull myself together, think of something to do. I had betrayed Angela to them, and I was not going to let this happen to her. But before I could speak, Claire touched my arm, asking me to be quiet for a moment.

She went around the desk and sat down beside her father. She folded her hands to stop their shaking, and with an extraordinary effort she summoned up her accustomed low and reasonable voice.

"He's making you an accomplice, Dad," she said slowly. "He can . . . do without Angela now because he knows you're the source. And from now on you'll be in his power. Dad, it's only going to get worse unless you stop it!"

He turned, staring at her wide-eyed. As always she had known the right thing to say, known that he would respond only to the threat against himself. In a matter of minutes I had come to despise Tom Cowan.

Claire swallowed and looked at her hands, and went on more slowly and softly than ever. "She expects to see you, but it'll be him, and he'll—he'll kill her!"

Her voice broke, finally, on the last words.

But she had made him realize what he had done. He shrank back into his chair, his face contorted.

"Just tell us where they're meeting," I said. "We can call the police. There's still time."

He jerked his head away from me. "No! It'll all come out then. I'll lose my position—they'll put me in prison!" His eyes sought Claire's pleadingly. "Claire, you can't let this happen to me."

She couldn't look at him now. Her shoulders shook as she struggled for self-possession.

"We won't bring the police into it. Just tell us where and we'll go out and—he won't do anything if there are witnesses." She was coaxing him as she would a child.

I felt the now familiar chill pass through me and leave me weak and shaking. I had been so badly frightened so often in the last two days; I didn't know where I would find the courage to go out in the cold night and face Tony again. But if it was the only way, I would have to do it.

Tom shook his head. "No, Claire, I won't let you go. He might—he might—"

I made a desperate effort and managed to speak. "She can stay here. I'll go alone. There's no reason for Claire to come."

I felt her eyes on me, but I was watching Cowan.

At last he spoke. "They're meeting on White Road. It's a little road off Forty-four, just beyond Wentworth."

I knew the road. I spun around and ran through the dark house toward the garage at the back, thinking frantically what to do. I could turn the lights on Tony, keep honking the horn, anything that might make him panic. If I was too late, Angela would die. And I would be a witness. I would be next.

Claire caught up with me in the kitchen and grasped my arm.

"Arthur, call the police."

I turned and stared at her. "But you told him—"

"We had to find out. I can't let you put yourself in danger for him."

There was pale light coming through the window now, enough to show her anguished face. I knew that if it was up to her, she would try to save her father.

"If I'm in time, there'll be no danger."

She gave a sob of relief, of hope, but at once she turned her face away. "No, you mustn't—" she managed to say, but then she broke off.

I stared at the phone hanging on the kitchen wall. She was leaving it up to me. If I picked up that phone, I would not have to go. I could stay in this safe, warm kitchen with Claire.

Until the police came and arrested her father. And then we would go out to Wentworth to get the files. Eventually I would have to testify that he had plotted murder.

I looked at Claire. I was surprised at the steadiness of my voice. "The police might not believe us right away. They might not know where to go. They'd be too late for sure."

Perhaps that was even true.

At once Claire turned to the door, grabbed the keys off a hook. I reached for them, but she shook her head.

"Claire, there's nothing you can do—"

"I have to go."

We looked at each other for a moment, and then I threw my arms around her. I felt the warmth of her body and wondered how I thought I could possibly have gone out and gotten in that car without her.

She threw open the door, and we stepped out into the dim, chilly garage. Claire moved toward the car, stopped suddenly, and knelt before a toolbox lying on the floor.

"Claire, we've got to hurry."

She didn't answer. I had no idea what she was after as she rummaged through the box. The garage door was open, and I looked out at the grey chill of the night's passing. It was six o'clock in the morning.

I remembered that sixty hours ago, I had intended to discard my life, throw it away as you throw away an empty can or a dead tennis ball. And now that I wanted my life so desperately, I would have to go out and risk it because of obligations, things I owed to Claire, to Angela.

Yet it might work out. I might be safe, have it all behind me, in an hour's time. I might be safe.

Claire got up from the toolbox, opened the car door, and got in. I jumped in on my side.

She turned to me. She had a gun. She held it lightly and carefully in both hands, as if it were a captured bird.

"You—you know something about these, don't you?"

I nodded and took it. It was a .45 automatic, Army issue, probably from Cowan's days in Korea. I released the clip: it was loaded. It was a simple, tough weapon, and I thought it would still work. It felt cold and heavy in my hands, and I held onto it all the way.

18

Cowan's car was enormous. A vast plain of bronze metal seeming broader than the road stretched before us. Claire accelerated to forty, and in the first turn the power steering tricked her—halfway through it the car's weight caught up with us like a blow and sent us slewing broadside across the road. The interior was so well soundproofed that I could hardly hear the screech of the tires as we skidded to a stop. Claire took her hands off the wheel and closed her eyes for a moment. Then she straightened the car out and continued on, steering carefully and quickly through the narrow streets, using both lanes.

She ran a light pulling onto 44 and stepped on the accelerator. We floated silently up to seventy and slipped along the broad highway, ignoring lights and an occasional car.

We roared past a Plymouth containing two men in fishing hats. It seemed extraordinary to me that they were going fishing, that all around us people were sleeping or making breakfast, getting on with their ordinary lives. It was six o'clock Saturday morning, just another Saturday morning. The Plymouth honked as we went by; they were angry at us for going so fast.

A sign that read WENTWORTH MEMORIAL HOSPITAL slipped by on the right. That woke me up; I had been leaning forward tensely out of the soft seat, cradling the pistol in my hands and thinking about nothing.

But White Road was only a few miles beyond Wentworth. I had to start planning.

Cowan had told Angela he would meet her. But he had refused to come to her apartment or to allow her to come to his house. Instead he had made her drive out to this deserted road. For a moment I cherished the hope that she would grow suspicious and not show up. She had the morphine; she was only returning the pills for Tom's sake—and mine. I closed my eyes under a wave of shame and prayed that she would not die on account of her own generosity.

We topped a hill, and at the bottom I saw a little road leading off to the right and a sign. I couldn't remember exactly, and I hoped it would not read White Road. I knew that speed was our only chance, but still I hoped that it wasn't White Road.

It was. Claire slowed and turned in.

As we drove the sky had turned from grey to the mildest shade of blue. Just above the hills to the east the sun had risen, a small, red-orange disc. We drove through a little copse of birches and started up a bare hillside.

We passed a wooden sign bearing the name of a big real-estate developer and, in italic script, the words *Coming soon—Thornycroft Hill Trails.* Lining the road as it climbed the hill were big piles of crumbling, muddy earth on lots that had been scraped bare but for little clumps of weeds. On some of them stood concrete foundations surrounded by deep ditches like moats, on others half-completed houses, skeletons of bright, new boards partially covered in a black sheathing material. All around lay large, empty boxes and piles of lumber under canvas tarps.

Near the top of the hill the road widened into a turning circle and ended. On the slope above it were two nearly finished houses. Parked in front of one of them, about twenty feet off the road, was a car, a white Volkswagen.

I thought: he's done it; he's murdered her and gotten away. I felt a wave of sorrow and anger and, shamefully, relief. We were too late; there was nothing we could do.

Claire had seen the car, too. "Is it possible—is it possible he hasn't gotten here yet?"

I nodded; it was possible. Very likely Angela lived near here because she worked at Wentworth. Maybe she had arrived first. Maybe Tony had taken a wrong turn; he didn't know Hartford. Right now Angela might be sitting in that car, alive, looking down at us, at Tom's car.

But Tony would get here at any minute. Even now he might be turning off the highway a half mile behind us.

We drew level with the Volkswagen, and Claire stopped. I threw open the door and jumped out. "Turn the car around!" I shouted. "If you see Tony coming, step on it and get out of here!"

"But you'll—"

I flung the door closed, cutting her off. There was no time to talk. I wanted to reach Angela, warn her, and get away, fast.

I ran hard up the bare, muddy hill, nearly tripping over the scars left by the treads of bulldozers. I could see Angela through the back window. She was leaning against the door on the driver's side.

I reached the door, opened it. She fell toward me and I caught her by the shoulder. At once I knew that we were wrong, that Tony had been here and done his work. Fearfully I looked at her, searching for the gunshot wound, the dark-red widening stain.

There was none. But her coat had been dragged off on the right side, her sleeve rolled up. I looked at the passenger seat and saw a syringe lying there, empty. I lifted her head and brushed aside her long golden hair. Horribly, her skin was almost blue. I stood holding her for a moment, shocked and still, and I could hear her breathing—light, irregular. She was slowly suffocating.

At last I came to understand. Tony was too smart, too cool, to shoot her cleanly and run. He had gotten here first, and surprised her, knocked her unconscious. Then he had injected her with a lethal dose of morphine. When the police found her they would see the little cluster of needle marks on her arm and know she was an addict. They would think she had taken an accidental overdose. Tony would get away with it.

Gently I laid her back against the seat and closed the door. And then I looked up, and fear closed around my chest with an iron grip.

Behind the slatlike structure of the unfinished house to my left a big blue car was parked, hidden from the road. Tony had not gotten away yet.

I backed up a step, then turned and started to run.

Claire's car was turned around and waiting at the foot of the slope. I could see her, looking anxiously up at me through the window.

I was only a dozen feet away when the shot rang out.

I threw myself down with a great sob of pain. I was so frightened that for a moment I didn't even understand that I wasn't hit. I just lay in the mud, flailing my arms and legs, trying to crawl, gasping like a child after a bad fall.

At last I made it to the cover of a pile of lumber, just as the gun roared again. Splinters bit into my hand. He had missed me by a foot. Vaguely I wondered how he had missed me on the first shot. And then I realized that he had not been aiming at me.

I looked down at the car. There was a tracery of tracks in the safety glass of the back window, and I could see Claire's head, fallen forward against the steering wheel.

For a moment I could not believe it, and then I knew that she was dead, and I slumped down on my hands and knees, and wept helplessly.

Claire had believed, long after it was too late, that everything would turn out all right, that we could save Angela and get Tom off. She always believed that she could save any situation by her own efforts, and it had cost her her life.

But I could not tell myself that. It was my fault for giving into the hope in her eyes and telling her we did not have to go to the police. I thought of Angela, slowly, quietly dying not ten feet away. That was my fault, too.

My thoughts moved in dark, ragged circles of bitterness and self-hatred. And I hated the others, too— Jim Siegel, for letting himself be used and not admitting it; Tom, for setting up the whole mechanism of secrecy that had cause me to be so disastrously wrong; and even Angela, for being an addict and beginning all of this. For what seemed a long time I knelt in the cold mud with my head in my hands, weeping and choking.

Then I heard footsteps approaching over the sodden ground. Tony. Coming to finish me off. Dimly I realized that he had shot Claire first because she had the car. Now he could take me at his leisure.

And that did it—the realization of the cold methodical cruelty of the man. I stopped blaming Angela, and Tom, and Jim, and Claire, and myself. We had all been put in impossible positions, one after the other, and we had yielded to our weaknesses and our needs, and then had been paralyzed by our sense of decency and of our shortcomings. But this man had no sense of decency. He had caused it all, finally, forcing us to make hard decisions, taking advantage of our wrong choices, our foolishness, our weaknesses. And in his blind, assertive egotism he felt no guilt at all.

I looked at the gun in my hand; I had forgotten I

was carrying it. I pulled back the slide and let it go, watching the fat golden bullet slip into the chamber.

It's not our fault, I thought. It's yours. Your hard selfishness has cut us to pieces and carried you through without a scratch. But it won't work this time. I'm going to kill you for what you've done, for using our guilt and feeling none yourself. I'm going to kill you now.

I stood up.

He was so close—less than thirty feet away. I could see those eyes as they fell on me; the short, wide-nostriled nose; the set, cruel smile; the gold-ringed hand holding the black revolver.

My arm went up smooth and steady, and Tony saw that I had a gun and jerked his own up.

There is a strange thing about firing a gun: at the last moment, it cannot be a conscious act. If you pull the trigger, the barrel jolts a fraction of an inch, and you miss. You must slowly tighten your finger, not knowing when the gun will go off.

Tony knew that if he missed me I would kill him, that he had only one chance. He pulled the trigger.

I heard the bullet slap into the wood beside me, and through the blades of my sight I watched him frantically dragging his gun level.

The automatic roared and snapped my wrist up and back. I pulled it down and aimed again.

Tony was a smaller target now. He was on his knees, sagging to the ground. The automatic went off again, and his head jerked up and back in an arc of red mist, and he toppled over.

I let the gun slip from my hand and turned away. In the silence I could hear the drone of the engine of Claire's car. I started down the slope and fell in the mud. It took me a long time to get up. I was covered with mud now, and I felt cold.

I reached the road and walked slowly up behind

the car. The bullet had left a ring of crumbled safety glass, like frost, around the hole, and sent cracks running the length of the window.

Eventually I came level with the driver's door and dragged my head up to look in.

The wound did not show; the bullet must have hit her in the forehead as she turned to look up at me, and her face was pressed against the rim of the steering wheel and hidden by her thick, golden-brown hair.

I opened the door and put my hands on her warm shoulders, gently pulling her back against the seat and raising her head.

There was so little blood; the wound across her forehead was just a scrape, a red smear, as if she had fallen off a bicycle and skinned herself.

It took me a long time to realize that she was breathing—that Tony had not calculated on the deflection from the safety glass, that the bullet had just scratched her, had missed killing her by two inches.

"You're lookin' a lot better now, fellah," said the friendly state trooper later that day. "When we first saw you, you were walkin' in circles around that car, shakin' like a leaf, and you didn't know what the hell was goin' on."

19

Arthur Lavien, Sr., approached and laid a tray before me. It bore a cup of coffee for himself, and orange juice, bacon, eggs, and toast for me. It was my first meal in forty hours, and I devoured it in religious silence.

At last I finished and looked up at him.

"They wanted to have a tray brought to your room, but I thought it was better for you to get out of there."

I nodded. "It was pretty rough for a while."

He gave his weary, professional half smile. The ways of the law, which he knew so well, rather amused him. "I suppose you thought they would shake your hand and send you off for a rest in the Bahamas."

"I don't know about that, but I didn't think they'd try to arrest me."

The wrinkles gathered on his broad forehead. "In fact, if they could have put you under arrest immediately, it would have been much easier for you. But they didn't know what to do." He shook his head; unprofessionalism always caused him pain. "Hence that shambles this morning."

He reached into the inside pocket of his suit—an elegantly muted-grey glen plaid—and brought out one of his trim, dollar-a-piece Jamaican cigars. He held it up to me and I nodded, and he took a cutter out of his vest pocket, clipped a slice out of it, and handed it to me.

"Some of them are still rather hot on the idea of

putting you away, but I think I've managed to dissuade them." He smiled to himself, no doubt remembering with pleasure the arguments he had used.

I had been glad to see Arthur Lavien, Sr., when he walked in that morning. An hour before, I had come to a few of my senses—I seemed to be heavily doped up—to find myself sitting in a little cubicle in Wentworth's emergency room, surrounded by cops in uniforms of every hue and a few men in suits, who were the meanest of all. They kept asking me impossibly complex questions. I seemed to know the answers, but right then I couldn't remember them. Whenever I did say something, one of the plainclothesmen would interrupt indignantly, "Are you aware—" and tell me I had committed some crime and threaten to arrest me. So I decided to ignore them and continue my fascinating conversation with the young resident who was pulling splinters out of my right hand.

"She's all right?"

"Oh, yes. Just a mild concussion. She should regain consciousness soon."

"She's all right then?"

I understood him, but I wanted him to keep saying it.

The boys in blue and tan were beginning to get really impatient with me when my father walked in. He looked at them disdainfully over the rims of his reading glasses, a confident and utterly humorless smile on his lips. Incongruously, he was carrying a fine silk dressing gown over his arm.

In a calm, deliberate tone—the familiar tone that suggested he knew better than anyone else what was going on—he cleared the room. Then he turned to me and stiffly held out the robe.

"You'll look a good deal better in this."

I knew what he meant. My clothes, acrid and stiff with mud, blood, and three days' worth of cold sweat, lay in a corner of the room. I was glad to have them off, but the nurses had put me in one of those backless hospital gowns, and I felt defenseless and a little silly. Draped in the silken folds of his dressing gown, I felt much more able to deal with things.

He sat down facing me, his head tilted back as usual so that his eyes were hidden behind the frames of his glasses, and began to ask questions in a careful, reasonable sequence. As I answered them, it all came back to me. But I did not relive the last twenty-four hours as I told the story; I was too tired. It was as if it had all happened to somebody else.

When he was satisfied, he brought a few selected cops back in, and I did a great deal of nodding as he explained it all to them. He made me sound perceptive and judicious, hardly mentioned Claire at all, and downplayed Jim's part in it. He was not so easy on Cowan. When the police started to ask inconvenient questions, he hinted to the resident that medical considerations forbade my tiring myself. The resident firmly agreed, and we were rid of the law. For a while.

Now we sat in Wentworth's cafeteria, with the sun streaming through the big windows, making the green-plastic chairs gleam. I remembered that I had met Claire here.

My father was watching the thick blue smoke from his cigar drift in the currents from a window. There were questions I had to ask him, even though I did not want to hear the answers.

"Dad—I suppose Angela—"

He nodded. "She was dead when the ambulance arrived."

I shifted unhappily in my chair. I had known the moment I saw her that she was beyond help. I wondered why it was that kind, yielding people like her always put themselves at the mercy of thoughtless, selfish people like Tony and Tom.

Tom.

"What about Dr. Cowan? Have they arrested him yet?"

"Yes."

"At his house?"

Again he was staring thoughtfully into the smoke. "No. Here."

"Here?"

"He arrived at work as usual today. They told him his daughter was in the emergency room, and he came down to see her. They arrested him there."

I shuddered. It was just as well that Claire had been unconscious.

"How did he react?"

My father gestured vaguely with his cigar. "It seemed as if he couldn't believe it."

I nodded. "He never could believe it."

My father did something unusual then. He took off his glasses and looked at me.

"He was only guilty of being afraid, really. Once one gets into a situation like that, the fear grows and grows, drives one to do desperate things. It could happen to anybody."

I felt my old urge to argue with him. "It couldn't happen to you."

He considered that in his even-handed legal way. And then he looked at me and smiled. His humor could never be anything but ironic, and he smiled only when he had won a point.

And he had won this one. I was admitting to him that I had been wrong about everything, about what had happened and who was guilty.

"It seems you have seen the error of your ways," he said.

I nodded. I had seen a calculated plan in what was really a shambles of guilt and confusion. I had preferred to suspect my father for his cold, indifferent rationality and impregnable complacency. I used to like Tom Cowan for lacking these qualities, and I had not seen how dangerous his moody, irresponsible character was.

I looked into my father's narrowed grey-green eyes. "Yes," I told him. "I've seen the error of my ways. And so have you."

He raised his arched eyebrows.

"You didn't have to come up here today. This had nothing to do with you."

Again he coolly weighed the argument. "You are my son, after all—"

"I thought you'd washed your hands of me three years ago."

We exchanged a long, conscious look; then he conceded the point with an almost imperceptible nod, and looked away.

That was it. That was all there was to his reconciliation with his son. It would never occur to him to apologize for throwing me out of college; he thought his arguments had been quite valid. He could not even say that he was glad that I was alive today.

I looked at him and wondered how in the past he could so fill me with rage and despair. American corporations needed someone to master the law for them; and in exchange for warmth and leisure, for a real life, they had offered him work he enjoyed and a big office and a hundred thousand a year. He was not very interested in life anyway, so he had taken the deal, and the accumulation of so much expertise and wealth had duly smothered his feelings. Now I saw him as a lonely, narrow, but rather decent middle-aged man who tried to do what his reason told him was right, if he had the time. I felt sorry for him. I wondered why I had always blamed my life on him, and why I had even tried to destroy it. Suddenly, completely, I was free of my father and his failings.

We smoked in silence for a while; we never had much to say to each other. After a few minutes a white-coated man walked through the doors, looking around.

My father waved to him, and he came over to the table.

"She's coming out of it now?"

"Shortly. She's mildly sedated, but she'll be fully conscious."

"Thank you."

The man smiled and turned away, with a fleeting, wary glance at me. I was getting a lot of glances like that.

My father rose, clearing his throat. "I thought, and Dr. Berry agrees, that someone should be with Claire when she comes around, and you're quite obviously the man for the job."

He could never use the vocabulary of emotion, but he had the right idea. I stood and thanked him. He nodded and told me he had to return to the office.

Outside the cafeteria door a young nurse caught up with me.

"Mr. Lavien," she said firmly, "the doctor says you're to return to your room at once. You need to rest."

"I will," I said. "I'll be there in about fifteen minutes."

She looked as if she was about to call an orderly, so I explained it to her. Everyone in Wentworth knew some of the story by now.

"Oh, of course. I suppose that's all right—just for a few minutes." But she hesitated, unwilling to leave her mission completely unaccomplished. "Anyway, the doctor says you're to take this. It's to make you drowsy."

She held out a cup of water and a stiff paper container like a large thimble. Inside it there was a small, light-blue capsule. Amytal.

I popped it and went upstairs to be with Claire.

Dell Bestsellers

- [ ] **INVASION OF THE BODY SNATCHERS**
  by Jack Finney $1.95 (14317-9)
- [ ] **MY MOTHER/MY SELF** by Nancy Friday....$2.50 (15663-7)
- [ ] **THE IMMIGRANTS** by Howard Fast $2.75 (14175-3)
- [ ] **BEGGARMAN, THIEF** by Irwin Shaw $2.75 (10701-6)
- [ ] **THE BLACK SWAN** by Day Taylor $2.25 (10611-7)
- [ ] **THE PROMISE** by Danielle Steele based on
  a screenplay by Garry Michael White $1.95 (17079-6)
- [ ] **MAGIC** by William Goldman $2.25 (15141-4)
- [ ] **THE BOYS FROM BRAZIL** by Ira Levin $2.25 (10760-1)
- [ ] **PEARL** by Stirling Silliphant $2.50 (16987-9)
- [ ] **BUCK ROGERS IN THE 25th CENTURY**
  by Richard A. Lupoff $1.95 (10843-8)
- [ ] **COMES A HORSEMAN**
  by Dennis Lynton Clark $1.95 (11509-4)
- [ ] **TARIFA** by Elizabeth Tebbets Taylor $2.25 (18546-7)
- [ ] **PUNISH THE SINNERS** by John Saul $1.95 (17084-2)
- [ ] **SCARLET SHADOWS** by Emma Drummond $2.25 (17812-6)
- [ ] **FLAMES OF DESIRE** by Vanessa Royall $1.95 (15077-9)
- [ ] **STOP RUNNING SCARED**
  by Herbert Fensterheim Ph.D. & Jean Baer $2.25 (17734-0)
- [ ] **THE REDBOOK REPORT
  ON FEMALE SEXUALITY**
  by Carol Tavris and Susan Sadd $1.95 (17342-6)
- [ ] **THE FAR CALL** by Gordon R. Dickson $1.95 (12284-8)